The Librarian

Little Boy Lost

Eric Hobbs

Eric Hobbs
4026 Highland Springs Drive
Kokomo, IN 46902

www.erichobbsonline.com

Publisher's Note: This is a work of fiction. Names, characters, places, and incidents are a product of the author's imagination. Locales and public names are sometimes used for atmospheric purposes. Any resemblance to actual people, living or dead, or to businesses, companies, events, institutions, or locales is completely coincidental.

Book design © 2013, BookDesignTemplates.com

Ordering Information: Special discounts are available on quantity purchases by corporations, associations, and others. For details, contact the publisher at the address above.

Kokomo, IN / Eric Hobbs – First Edition

ISBN 978-0-6926703-9-2

Printed in the United States of America

For mom,
who gave me all the tools.

PROLOGUE

LOCKE STOOD ON the beach looking for a smooth stone he could skip across Mermaid's Lagoon. He wouldn't find one, of course. He knew that much. He'd looked for the stone more times than he could count. More times than *anyone* could count, really. And yet, he looked for the stone each time his adventures led him here. It was the curse of living a life controlled by words on a page.

Eventually, like always, he dug a rough chunk of rock from the black sand and tossed it into the lagoon. It landed with a heavy splash that sent ripples racing across the water's surface. He stood and watched. Then, right on schedule—

"Why are you just standing around?" someone asked in an excited tone.

Locke turned to find Nibs approaching. Like Locke, Nibs was a Lost Boy. His clothes were thrown together for dramatic effect: a tattered tuxedo jacket paired with a black top hat that was wrinkled up like an accordion.

"C'mon!" he exclaimed. "Peter's a-waitin!"

Locke watched him scurry away. Nibs had one hand on the brim of his hat while the other was wrapped around the handle of a scuffed briefcase. He stumbled over an exposed tree root along the way, just as he'd done the time before and the time before that.

Right on cue, a streak of yellow light cut through the air toward Locke. It circled him twice and left a trail of golden dust hanging in the air around him. A moment later, Locke felt Tinkerbell's tiny hands pushing on his back.

"I'm going, Tink! Relax, would ya?"

She came around to face him, stopping to hover just inches from his face. A true fairy, Tinkerbell was no larger than the smallest finger on Locke's hand. Her blonde hair was tied in a messy bun that exposed her pointed ears. She wore a tiny green dress that was open in the back to accommodate wings that moved so fast they were nothing but a blur.

"I said—"

Tink flipped Locke on the nose before he could finish then flew away. Locke shook his head and grinned. He always fell for that. Locke was the only one who knew how each of their adventures would unfold; the only one who understood they were trapped in a cycle that would never end. Usually this knowledge left him feeling morose and alone, but there were times even he had to laugh.

Locke started down the shore, following the trail of fairy dust as it began to dissipate. The other Lost Boys were climbing into a small rowboat just ahead of him. All but one. One of the boys was floating in mid-air with a hand on each hip. The redhead had a face full of freckles and was wearing a wide, mischievous grin. His peculiar clothes were tailored from autumn leaves and cobwebs.

His name was Peter Pan.

Peter gestured to the briefcase. "That it?"

Nibs nodded as he climbed into the boat.

"Good," Peter said excitedly. "Don't get it wet."

"What do ya take me for, Peter? I know better than that."

"Well," Peter began, "I'm just reminding you."

"I don't need no remindin'."

Locke waited for Peter to lower himself into the boat then pushed it away from shore and hopped into the dinghy. He settled into a seat beside two boys known only as the Twins.

"Careful," Peter said. "The mermaids will pull you under if you give them a chance." Locke looked nervously into the water as it passed beneath the boat. Why did Peter always have to remind him of that?

The kids sat in silence as Tootles rowed the boat out of Mermaid's Lagoon before turning north toward Skull Rock. There, anchored near the creepy rock formation deserving of its name, was Captain Hook's ship.

"There she is," Peter called. "The Jolly Roger."

The boat's ancient wood seemed to moan as the Jolly Roger rocked back-and-forth. The galleon-style ship was a dark vessel: a wooden behemoth with four giant sails, a crew of thirty men, and a dozen guns. A black flag decorated with a white skull-and-crossbones flew proudly atop the ship's tallest mast.

Peter pointed to a skinny man stationed in the ship's lookout. "Take care of that, Tink."

The order was barely off his lips before Tinkerbell darted away, seized the pirate's telescope, and used it to knock him unconscious.

Tootles pulled his oars into the boat. Everyone kept their eyes fixed on Hook's ship as the rowboat slowed to a stop near a rusted chain that extended from a porthole in the ship's hull before disappearing into the water below. Peter led the way, climbing the chain then throwing his leg over the rail when he reached the ship's deck. Once the others were aboard, Peter motioned toward a rickety staircase that led below.

"This way," he whispered.

They tiptoed down the steps. The snorting and snoring of sleeping pirates echoed all around them. Just knowing the scoundrels were that close was enough to put a few of the Lost Boys on edge.

Eventually, the small group followed Peter into a room that was filled floor-to-ceiling with broken clocks. Alarm clocks, grandfather clocks, pocket watches, and more. They sat shoved together on shelves and on tables. There were even piles of them on the floor. Hundreds of timepieces. Maybe more. All of them apparently broken with a rubber mallet that was leaning against the wall as if tired after a long day's work.

"This is going to be so great," Peter giggled.

Nibs was already on his knees, ready to open the briefcase he'd brought with them.

Peter pulled his sword from its sheath and pretended to fence a pirate that wasn't there. "Hurry up! Before we get caught, and I have to teach Hook another lesson."

"I'm going, I'm going." Nibs popped the locks and carefully removed an antique cuckoo clock from inside the case. It was a beautiful piece. Its face was made of ivory with inlaid gold numbers. The tiny doors that opened on the hour were intricately carved from the finest woods in Neverland.

Nibs wound the clock with a golden key then hid it in a nook behind several of the broken clocks already there.

The Lost Boys began to laugh.

Peter put a finger to his lips. "Shh! Listen!"

The room fell silent except for the faint sounds of the hidden clock.

Tik, tik, tik.

"Perfect," Peter said. "Let's go."

They hurried out the door and started down the hall only to stop when the gruff sound of men's voices filtered down from atop the stairs – just as Locke knew it would.

Nibs trembled. "Is that—"

"Hook," Peter finished. "C'mon. In here."

Peter opened a nearby closet and his crew piled inside. He left the door cracked just enough so he could watch as the pirates stormed by.

"It's Hook, alright. And Smee."

Captain James Hook was a towering man with a menacing stare. His black hair flowed down his back in long curls. He wore a red coat with black trim and golden tassels. His three-cornered hat bore a long white feather extending well past its brim. And, of course, there was a large silver hook in the place that previously belonged to his right hand.

"I don't understand, capt'n."

"That doesn't surprise me, Smee."

The man with Hook wasn't nearly as formidable. Smee was a short, disheveled man who looked like he'd just rolled out of bed. His pale belly fell over his belt and peeked out from beneath his shirt.

"How can we put our trust in some man we don't know?"

"But I *do* know him, Smee. I told you. I met him *today*."

"Oh," Smee said. "Of course. It's just—"

The pirate came to an abrupt halt when Hook grabbed him by the shirt and pinned him to the wall. Hook held Smee in place and squinted his eyes with fury.

"W-w-what you d-doing there, capt'n?"

"Do you hear that, Smee?"

"I don't hear a t'ing. C-could you l-let me go?"

Hook released him then started toward the stairs. "Wake the men! I think that wretched crocodile has come to finish me off! Well, he won't get me without a fight! I promise you that much, Smee! I..." He didn't finish.

"Capt'n?"

The pirate rushed into the clock room without answering.

"Where ya goin', capt'n?"

"Help me find it, Smee!"

Smee stumbled in after him.

"Of course, capt'n. I'll help you with anything. You know that. But... if I may... what... what are we looking for?"

"You fool! Don't you hear it? *A clock!*"

Smee cringed. "But sir, all-o-these clocks have been destroyed. You made sure—"

He stopped short, his ears at attention.

Tik, tik, tik.

"Wait," Smee said. "I think I do hear a-somethin, capt'n."

Hook slid across the room and grabbed the mallet. He swung it wildly, happy to let it bash anything within reach. Smee had to duck the mallet more than once as shards of shattered clocks rained down around him. In the closet, Peter slapped both hands across his mouth to keep from laughing.

"Did I get it? Did I get it, Smee?!"

"Capt'n! Stop!"

Hook stopped just long enough to listen. His hat had shifted so that it sat lopsided on his head. The hint of a dark smile appeared on his face. But then...

Tik, tik, tik.

Hook gave a furious growl and let the mallet fly.

"No, capt'n! Please!"

"Someone will walk the plank for this outrage! I swear it!"

He hit everything in his path. He broke shelves. He shattered a window. Once, his foot slipped and the mallet tore a hole through the wooden floor at his feet.

Peter couldn't hold it in any longer. A rush of laughter exploded out of him. Luckily, it went unheard beneath Hook's rage.

Smee backed into a corner for safety. However, he quickly found the more steps he took, the louder the clock's ticking became. Smee began digging through the clocks on a nearby shelf. He spotted the cuckoo clock and saw that its second hand was moving briskly past the golden numbers on its face.

"Capt'n?"

Hook wheeled around in anger.

Smee held the clock out to him with trembling hands.

Tik, tik, tik.

"That's it?"

Smee nodded nervously.

"Why, it looks brand new," Hook said. "Peter Pan did this, Smee. That clock wasn't in this room before. Oh my! Such bad form to play on an adversary's fears like this. Bad form, Peter. Truly!"

"Really, capt'n? It doesn't seem that bad to me. Remember that time we—"

"Smee?"

"Yes, sir?"

"Did I say it's bad form?"

"Well... umm... yes, capt'n."

"*Then it's bad form!*" the pirate screamed.

Smee shrunk away.

Hook pointed to a table near the window. "Put it there."

Smee did as he was told.

"The man I met? He's going to help us put an end to these childish games. This war with Peter Pan has gone on too long." He raised the mallet, choking down on its handle for control. "I'm going to finish Pan if it's the last thing I do."

He brought the hammer down, and the clock split in two. The yellow bird inside croaked as it spilled through the clock's doors on a bent spring. When he saw it, Hook flattened the bird for good measure then tossed the mallet aside and stormed out of the room. "Get one of the men to clean this up."

"Yes, capt'n. Right away."

Peter waited until the men were up the stairs and out of sight before turning to his friends. "That's it, Lost Boys. Show's over."

The kids tumbled out of the closet and into the clock room where Peter began ushering them through a tiny window one at a time. Locke took a post near the door to make sure no one came down the hall as his friends made their escape. Not that anyone would. No one *ever* came. He'd stood the post more times than he could count. More times than *anyone* could count and he'd never—

Locke's heart nearly leapt from his chest when Hook and Smee came barging down the steps once more.

"I'm going to show you what I'm talking about, Smee. Then you'll understand."

Locke pulled the door shut and let the pirates pass. When they were gone he quickly checked on the others then crept out of the room. He heard muffled voices coming from Hook's quarters at the end of the hall. He inched forward and put his ear to the door. He could hear everything.

"He told me he's from America. Does that make sense to you, Smee? He called it the *real* world."

Locke furrowed his brow, his thoughts running fast and wild. He'd met a man who claimed to be from the real world, too. In fact, he'd *been* to the real world himself. It was there that he'd learned the truth: everything in Neverland was a lie. Neverland was nothing more than a fictional place. The people in Neverland didn't have control over their lives. It was all just words on the page. The story never changed. It was always the same. Every single time.

Until it wasn't.

"I don't understand," Smee said. "I thought *this* was the real world. I don't see how one world can be any more real than the next. That don't make no sense."

"Well, that's what the man said. He said he's from a land where battles aren't won with swords and canons. In *his world* you can be victorious with the simple push of a button."

"Oh," Smee said, thinking. Then: "What's a button? Like the button on your shirt?"

"No! You fool! A button can... well... it... it's... *it's from the real world!* Stop asking so many questions! Didn't you hear me? We can finally bring this war to an end. With his help, we can win."

"What if it's a double-cross?"

"Then I'll run him through!"

Embarrassed by his outburst, Hook took a deep breath. He smoothed his coat with both hands and straightened his hat.

"He gave me something. Proof he comes from a place far from here, a world where children know their place, I'm sure."

Locke pushed the door open just a hair so he could see into the cabin. He watched Hook sit down behind a large desk and pull open one of its drawers. The pirate took something from inside and handed it to Smee.

"Careful," Hook whispered. "Careful."

Smee studied the tiny device with curiosity before finally speaking up. "Wow, capt'n. It's glorious!" He cocked his head to the side. "What is it?"

"Well... Smee... it's... it's... it's a button, of course!" Hook made a flourish with his hand as if presenting something quite grand.

"Oh! Of course, capt'n. I knew that."

The two men grinned wickedly as Smee held the "button" to the flame of a candle on Hook's desk for a better look.

Locke gasped. It was like nothing he'd ever seen. It was black and smooth and forged into the shape of rectangle with rounded corners. The device was made from a material that was foreign to Locke. It truly looked like something from another world. While he had no idea what the "button" was, he knew one thing for certain: it had no business in Neverland.

Locke backed away from the door. It had been so long since his trip into the real world; so long since the old man asked him to become Neverland's Watcher. He'd been watching Neverland's story unfold for years, longer even, so long in fact that he thought he was waiting for something that would never come. But now it was finally here. Someone had thrown a stone into Neverland and there was no telling just how far the ripples of change might spread.

CHAPTER 1

WESLEY STOPPED ON the last step before climbing off the bus and gaped at the building before him. He'd heard stories about the library since his move to Astoria, but now it was looming over him like a stone dinosaur from another age. The old building looked strangely out-of-place in Astoria's modern skyline. It looked like a castle. Tall, arched windows were set in the upper floors. There was a weathervane perched atop the roof that looked like a leaping stag. For a moment, Wes thought he saw movement in one of the windows but checked again and saw nothing there. Still, it was the library of his dreams. Wesley imagined an ancient time, centuries ago, long before the building became Astoria's library, when armies from around the world took turns storming the gate, each determined to obtain the treasures hidden within. It was that kind of place. It stirred something inside of him.

Put more simply: Wesley Bates was in awe.

"Don't just stand there, Bates. Move!"

Before he could react, someone shoved Wes from behind so he fell from the step and tumbled to the concrete. He fell hard, skinning his knee as his backpack spilled its contents on the ground beside him.

Behind him, a few kids laughed at Wesley's expense. He looked up to find Randy Stanford standing over him. He was sporting the same crooked grin he always wore in moments like this. Caleb Rodriguez was with him. No surprise there. But the dozen kids waiting to get off the bus were staring at Wesley, too. Somehow seeing Randy's audience made Wesley's knee hurt even worse.

Already off the bus, Taylor Morales hurried over to help Wesley collect his things. "What's your problem, Randy? He didn't do anything to you."

"You know," Randy began, "I don't know which is worse: that he's your boyfriend, or that he's such a wuss *you* have to stand up for *him*."

Taylor was about to respond when their chaperone stepped in. "People want to get off the bus. Let's move. And Randy, I'd like a word." Dressed in a slate-colored suit, Douglas Stanford gestured for his son to join him.

"Jeez, Dad! I'm coming!" Randy made a show of stepping over Wesley and Tay as he started down the sidewalk to join the students clustered near the library's wrought-iron gate. At least Caleb was nice enough to walk around.

Wesley fought tears as he put the rest of his things in his bag.

"You okay?"

"Think Ally Asthma will let me take a hit from her inhaler?"

"Don't call her that," Taylor scolded with a grin.

The friends rose to their feet. Wesley slung his bag over one shoulder and pushed his glasses up on his nose. Taylor shifted her gaze to their chaperone who was having a stern conversation with his son.

"*That's* Randy's dad?"

"I guess."

"Weird. He's never chaperoned before."

The kids watched as Douglas lectured his son. Wesley quietly hoped Randy wasn't getting in *too* much trouble. If so, Wesley knew he'd be the one to pay for it in the end.

Douglas shook his head in frustration, but the man's expression washed away when he noticed something in the parking lot directly behind Wesley and Tay.

Wesley turned and saw that a black sedan had just pulled to a stop behind the idling bus. The windows were heavily tinted, but Wesley could see a hulking figure in the car's back seat. Wesley waited for him to climb out of the car. When he didn't, Wes turned his attention back to Tay.

"You know I had it under control, right?"

"What?" Taylor asked.

"I don't need you stepping in for me. I can take care of myself."

He started to leave, but Taylor was persistent. She was *always* persistent.

"Why don't you say something, then? Or tell Ms. Easton? The only reason I ever say anything is because you don't. I mean, what's Randy gonna do? He's all talk. He's never—"

"Why do you care?" Wesley snapped. He wanted the words back the second they were gone.

Taylor lowered her eyes. "I... I don't know."

Ms. Easton was the last one off the bus. She hurried past Wesley and Taylor while instructing her class on how to proceed. "Does everyone have a partner?" Kids stood in pairs all around her. "Good! Be sure to stay with the group. No wandering off. You'll have plenty of time to explore *after* we've taken the tour."

She led her class down a long sidewalk through the library's gate and toward the stone building's entrance where she struggled to open one of the library's heavy, wooden doors. Looking back, she extended her free hand to show the kids her thumb and forefinger were just a sliver apart. "Let's remember this is a library. Let's use our *tiny voices* once inside."

She held the door open. Children entered the building one pair at a time.

Near the back, Wesley and Taylor exchanged awkward looks. "I'm sorry," Wesley muttered. "I didn't mean to yell at you like that. It's just..."

"I know, Wes."

It seemed she wasn't going to let him go any further down that path. He was grateful for that. He wasn't sure where it was heading anyway.

"Who's your partner?"

Taylor blushed. "Who's yours?"

The answer was obvious. The friends moved closer to one another, their shoulders brushing briefly as they took their place at the end of the line. Wesley looked up at the building as they entered the library. This time he was sure he spotted a shadow in the window: a wrinkled face looking down on the children below.

❖ ❖ ❖

The building's dim lobby was a stark contrast to the bright, sticky day outside. The library smelled of old leather and polished wood. There was something else, too: a fragrance Wesley couldn't put his finger on.

"Smells like history in here," Taylor whispered.

Wesley grinned. It was a strange way to describe the musty scent, but if Wesley needed to do it with a single word, "history" was just as good as any.

A chubby boy looked back at them with a silly grin. "Here's a little hist'ry for ya." The boy scrunched up his face and let a fart that cut through the small group like machine gun fire.

"Ugh! Jeff!" Taylor shoved the boy forward. He stumbled into the kids ahead of him, quickly earning their ire as well. "Why you gotta be so nasty?"

"That's enough," Ms. Easton said. "Let's keep it moving."

It took a moment for traffic to thin so Wesley and Taylor could continue into the library's main hall. Ms. Easton came in behind them. She smiled when she saw most of her students were staring in amazement as they took in their new surroundings.

The building was made of cool, dark stone: giant blocks, one on top of the other. Its architectural elements were cut from exotic woods. There were no signs of the modern world at all: no computers, no copy machines, no plastic chairs, or tables. Golden light radiated from polished brass fixtures on the walls powered by the whispering hiss of gas rather than electricity. The light was different somehow, soft and warm. The children gawked at everything around them. Nothing was ordinary. Everyone felt it. People didn't make buildings like this anymore. They hadn't in centuries.

An energetic woman in a short dress greeted them from the foot of a mammoth staircase that snaked its way to the building's second story. She waved them forward with a wide smile. "Thanks for coming. There's plenty of room. Come on in."

Many of the boys were immediately smitten with the young woman. She had a glow about her and smelled of vanilla. Ms. Easton took a place beside her. It was a great spot for keeping an eye on her students as they formed a semi-circle around their hostess. Randy's dad took a position near the back.

"My name's Hope," the woman explained. "I'm the assistant librarian here at Astoria Municipal. I'll be your guide on today's tour."

A boy in braces shoved a hand into the air before asking: "When do we meet the *weal* librawian?" He spoke with a lisp. Wesley wasn't sure if he was born with it or if it was the result of a mouth filled with metal.

"Ah! Well—"

"I hear he's like two hundred years old," someone interrupted. "Is that true?"

"Two hundred?" a kid with spiked hair asked. "Really? You're an idiot!"

"My dad said!"

"Yeah? Well, your dad's a freakin—"

Ms. Easton snapped her fingers. "Guys! Please!"

A pale girl took a shot from her inhaler before speaking up. "Oh yeah? Well, my sister, *she* told me The Librarian caught her friend's brother writing in one of the encyclopedias and no one ever saw him again."

"The Librarian?"

"No – *her friend's brother!*"

"Ally," their teacher interrupted. "Let's let Hope lead the tour. What do you say?"

Ms. Easton mouthed a quick apology to Hope that most of her students couldn't hear. Their young guide was just about to continue when someone else chimed in. This time it wasn't a student who interrupted...

"Urban legends about The Librarian have been floating around this town since I was a kid." Everyone turned in unison to hear Douglas Stanford speak. "Secret passages, buried treasure, magic powers – people act like we've got a wizard living right under our noses. You know what was so great about Willie Wonka's chocolate factory? When the kids finally got a look inside it was even more spectacular than they imagined. Trust me, The Librarian's no Willie Wonka. If you ever saw him you'd wonder why he isn't in the nursing home across the street."

"You've met him?" a young boy asked.

"Well, I—"

Hope cut him off. "Mr. Stanford is one of the developers hoping to tear the library down this summer and replace it with a *modern* facility."

"Really?" the boy asked. "Is that true?"

A look of contempt passed between the adults. When Douglas spoke again there was a hint of defeat in his voice. "I've met him, yeah."

"Now that we've got that out of the way..." Hope bent at the waist to look a few eager faces in the eye. "How many of you can tell me *who built* the Astoria Library?" The kids didn't respond. "No? Well, I'm guessing most of you already know this is the *oldest* building in our city. Does anyone know just *how old* the Astoria Library is?" Again, nothing. "That's very good. This is one time when *no* answer is just the answer I'm looking for." Most of the students were confused, but a few, Wesley and Taylor among them, were intrigued. "The truth is: no one knows for sure when the library was built or who built it. The building was already here –

abandoned – when Cutthroat Butler and his men came ashore in 1683."

This grabbed their attention. Kids in Astoria loved to hear about the notorious pirate who'd played such a major role in the city's history.

Seeing their interest piqued, Hope started away from their gathering point and moved deeper into the library. The kids quickly followed.

"Once visitors get past the building's old-world construction, the first thing most people notice are the literature displays scattered through our library's main hall." Hope pointed at an exhibit beside her. The display appeared somewhat out of place in a library. It looked more like something one would find in a museum. The display was simple enough: a square table topped with a heavy glass case. But the items inside were quite peculiar. There was a large, wooden chest in the center of the table that overflowed with gold coins and jewelry. A weathered map was placed beside the chest with the weight of a seventeenth-century pistol holding it in place. "These displays are unique to the Astoria Library," Hope continued. "You won't find them anywhere else in the world."

A young boy with freckled cheeks pressed his greasy nose to the glass. "Whoa! It looks so real."

Randy and Caleb sauntered by the boy. "Be glad it's not," Randy said.

"Why?"

"'Cause I'd steal every piece then kill anybody I thought might tell... *like you*."

The young boy didn't say another word the rest of their trip.

The next exhibit wasn't encased in glass. Instead, velvet ropes attached to brass posts kept visitors from interfering with its treasures: an Indian headdress, a dagger, an ominous metal hook, and the stuffed head of a crocodile, its mouth propped open by a ticking clock.

"Each diorama displays replica items from a classic piece of literature." Hope crossed the large room. There were more than a dozen displays in this part of the library alone. "Here's an interesting one." A long, chrome cylinder sat alongside a neatly folded black uniform in the next display. The cylinder was rigged to wear on one's back. A long coil of tubing extended from its base and connected the heavy pack to a metal device that looked like a gun. There was a helmet sitting just in front of the uniform. It was marked with the number 451. "This is the equipment used by firefighters in Ray Bradbury's *Fahrenheit 451*. Does anyone know what this book is about?"

Wesley shut Taylor down with a firm look before she had an opportunity to ask a question of her own. He'd read the book. She knew he had. Ray Bradbury was one of his idols. He dreamed he'd one day become an author who wrote just like him. But he wasn't about to admit that here – not in front of everyone.

Hope waited for an answer before continuing. "That book takes place in a future where it's illegal to read. Firefighters aren't paid to put out fires, they're paid to burn books."

Randy raised his hand.

"Yes?" Hope asked.

"If there were no books, what happened to all the libraries?"

"I suppose they got rid of those, too."

"Man," Randy snickered. "Where would Wesley eat lunch?"

A few kids laughed.

Wesley glared at Randy. He'd spent a lot of time in the mirror rehearing exactly what he would say and do when he finally stood up to Randy Stanford. He wanted to say something now, but the words caught in his throat. Something was holding him back. Typical. He never raised his hand in class; he never tried his best in gym; he never told his best friend how he felt about her.

Sometimes it felt like something was *always* holding him back.

"Take a moment to check out the other exhibits before we move into the Archives Room where you'll see we have the largest collection of first editions on the West Coast."

The children slowly began to disperse. Most students gravitated toward a *Wizard of Oz* display near a marble pillar in the center of the room. Others were drawn to a half-painted picket fence with a straw hat hanging from its gate. While Wesley was eager to explore, he waited to see where Randy and Caleb were heading first. There was a skylight in the main room's domed ceiling which allowed plenty of natural light into the building. But the sun also created a web of shadows that reached into the deepest recesses of the library. The building was a bully's playground: a collection of dark nooks and hidden crannies where a bad kid could get away with just about anything without being seen. Even with Randy's dad there, Wesley had to be safe.

If Randy and Caleb were heading one way, he would go the other.

With Taylor waiting, Wesley spotted the two boys near the *Peter Pan* display.

"He's an idiot," Taylor said matter-of-factly. "C'mon." They left the group and moved into a long aisle off the main hall. Towering bookcases flanked either side of them as they set out to explore on their own.

Wesley studied the mammoth books sitting on the top shelf. "How are you supposed to get some of these books down?" he wondered aloud. Most were blanketed with dust and missing the numeric label other books displayed on their spine. Some looked like they hadn't left the shelves in years.

"I'm sure they've got ladders or something."

Wesley glanced nervously over his shoulder as they walked deeper into the shadows, farther away from the skylight in the main hall.

"Wow!" Taylor gasped.

Wesley turned. Taylor was standing before a large piece of artwork hanging on the wall at the end of the aisle. Carved from a single piece of wood, it presented a breathtaking view of the ocean from cliffs high above a rocky beach. In the distance, a pirate ship attacked the inhabitants of a small island. Wes looked about and saw similar carvings capped the end of each aisle in the library.

"Why didn't she tell us about these?"

"We just got here," Wesley said. "Maybe she will."

"Maybe," Taylor said. She studied the intricacies of the carving. Each stone on the beach and every ripple of the water had been carved with incredible care and impossible detail. "Check out these mermaids!"

Taylor stepped aside to give Wes a better look. Sure enough, there were small mermaids swimming alongside the wooden ship.

"It's Neverland," Wesley said. He couldn't hide his excitement. Alone with Taylor, he didn't have to. "From *Peter Pan*. This one's Neverland."

"I saw the movie. I started the book but couldn't finish. Why can't they just write normal? That old English drives me nuts."

"That's how they talked back then."

Wesley hurried to the carving at the end of the next aisle. Equally beautiful, it featured several men in a hot air balloon flying over a snow-capped mountain range. The men were armed with rifles.

"What's that one?" Taylor asked.

"I don't know. Pretty cool, though."

The next carving offered them a look at a London street scene. Men in top hats traveled by horse-drawn carriages down a cobbled street. Wesley and Tay missed the sign above one of the doors: 221b Baker Street.

The children walked the aisles and took them in one at a time, marveling at their artistry. There were dragons and swordsmen, gorgeous landscapes and desolate wastelands. They came to the last carving on the wall a little quicker than either would have liked, but both immediately felt as if they'd saved the best for last.

"Oz," Taylor gasped. She stared at the piece for a long moment without speaking. "My mom... she used to read *Wizard of Oz* to me when I was little. It's one of my favorite memories of her. One of my *only* memories, I guess."

Taylor seemed lost in her thoughts. Wesley wasn't sure what to say. Her mother rarely came up, and when she did, it was the one thing that seemed to suck the wind from Taylor's sails. When she finally looked at the carving again, Wesley breathed a quiet sigh of relief.

Her eyes moved across the wood's grain. Every brick in the road leading through the hillside had been carved individually. Thousands of them. "Just one of these would take forever."

Wesley pointed to something that caught his eye. "Look at that little building on the left. It's darker than the rest." The artist had made deeper cuts in the wood to make this small piece of the Emerald City skyline more pronounced than the rest. Upon closer inspection, Wesley realized it was carved into the shape of a magic wand. The little building on the left wasn't a building at all.

"That's weird," Taylor said.

Wesley couldn't imagine why the artist would hide a wand in his work like this. But hadn't he seen something similar in the Neverland carving? He thought so but wasn't sure. He stepped forward, ready to lay his palm flat against the intricate carving when—

Someone grabbed his wrist from behind!

Wesley jumped with a start, yanking his hand free from a woman's powerful grip.

It was Hope, the assistant librarian.

"Please!" she said. "Don't touch the artwork."

"I'm sorry. I just—"

"It's fine," she explained. "Just... *don't*."

Wesley thought the woman was different now. Hope had greeted them so warmly before, offering nothing but pleasantries. But here, in this dark corner of the library, she seemed harsh and cold. Wesley found himself hoping Ms. Easton or Randy's dad was somewhere nearby.

"What are these things?" Taylor asked, the silence finally broken.

Hope kept her gaze on Wesley for a long moment before answering. "These? Well... just... it's artwork The Librarian's picked up in his travels around the world."

Wesley furrowed his brow. Again, she seemed different. She'd been so knowledgeable before, clear and confident in her every answer. Now she was stammering, hesitant and unsure.

"Where *is* The Librarian?" Taylor asked.

"Well," Hope began, "sometimes kids are lucky and get a glimpse of him near the end of their tour. You'll just have to keep your eyes peeled."

She placed a hand on Taylor's back and led her up the aisle – back into the library's main hall where the others were waiting. Both expected Wesley to follow, but he lagged behind, waiting for them to disappear around the corner before turning to face the Oz carving once more.

Wes noticed each carving was wrapped in an ornate frame carved directly into the wood. Also, each had a symbol near the artwork's upper edge: an open book with strange lines extending outward from its pages.

Wesley frowned. He was onto something, but he wasn't sure what.

Nearby, his teacher was calling the class together. "Line up, guys! C'mon!"

Wesley started down the aisle but stopped when he felt a cool draft on the back of his neck. Only it wasn't a draft. It felt like wind from an open window despite the fact there were no windows close by.

His neck prickled as he slowly turned. The wind was gusting now, and there was a strange light illuminating the next aisle.

The light brightened until it glowed white-hot. Wesley shielded his eyes with one hand while grabbing hold of a bookcase with the other as the wind whipped a few books off their shelves.

Birds called in the distance.

The smell of salt water filled the air.

Wesley dropped his hand. Beams of light were bending around the bookcase and into his aisle. Not beams, though. They were like long tentacles of light reaching around corners, exploring the world in a way that was anything but natural.

"Oh man! Oh man! Oh man!"

He slapped a hand over his eyes again, this time squeezing them shut as if this might grant him some added protection. He was sure one of those things was going to wrap around his ankle and drag him away. Or worse, maybe it would cut right through him. If that happened, he didn't want to watch.

But the wind subsided just as quickly as it had materialized. It carried the bird-calls and sea-salt air away with it. Wesley opened his eyes and found the strange, unexplained light was all that remained. It was dimming fast, its tentacles quickly retreating around the corner from where they'd come.

Every instinct told him to run: "Get out of here! Find Ms. Easton! Quick, kid! Go!" But Wes didn't listen. He took a single step toward the light, then another, until eventually he was giving chase, pursuing it around the corner as fast as his wiry legs would take him.

He came into the aisle just in time to watch the long beams of light recede into one of the carvings, fading away until there was nothing left of them at all.

"What the heck?"

Wesley stepped toward the artwork. It was the Neverland carving. Looking closely, he saw he'd been right – there was a small piece of the carving that was darker than the rest, a tree carved into the shape of a small dagger.

With no one to stop him this time, Wesley felt the dark imperfection with the tip of his finger. The wood was warm to the touch.

The carving had Wesley enraptured until he heard the jingle of movement behind him. He whipped about, convinced Randy and Caleb would be there to ruin his discovery. Instead, someone else was lurking in the shadows...

And this boy had a knife.

CHAPTER 2

THE WILD-HAIRED STRANGER was kneeling in the aisle behind Wesley. Sweat streamed down his olive-colored cheeks. A padlock dangled on a long cord that circled his neck. The ring of keys hanging from his belt jingled again as he rose to his feet. More than his appearance, there was something about the boy. Wes had trained himself to spot dangerous situations before they became impossible to avoid. For some reason this kid in tattered clothes reminded Wes of a coiled snake.

"Hi," Wesley began tentatively. "Who are—"

The stranger moved a hand to the dagger kept in a leather sheath on his belt.

"Where's The Librarian, boy? I need to speak with him at once."

Wesley froze. He knew any movement would see the knife unsheathed. He feared a poor answer might do the same so he kept his mouth shut.

The two stood in silence. Neither moved. Then, all at once, Taylor stormed down the aisle and caught both boys completely off guard.

"Why are you just standing there? Everyone else is already–"

Her eyes landed on the stranger just in time to see the startled boy lunge toward her. He grabbed Tay and shoved her across the room like she was stuffed with feathers and made from rags.

Taylor screamed. "What are you doing?"

But the boy didn't answer. Instead, he pulled his dagger and moved toward her, closer, ready to let the blade fly when–

Wesley stepped between them. He snatched the stranger's hand and guided the dagger away from his friend before pushing the boy away and pinning him to the wall. Taylor stared in disbelief. Even Wesley looked down at his hands like they belonged to someone else.

The boy shoved Wesley across the room. Wesley's skinny body slammed into a nearby desk. He fell to the floor. Books came crashing down around him.

Wesley looked up just in time to see his attacker coming down on him, the dagger raised above his head like the stinger on a scorpion. Quick to react, Wesley grabbed a book from the pile, held the book like a shield and squeezed his eyes shut. The knife sliced through the book, but the tip of its blade stopped just short of Wesley's throat when the dagger's hilt caught on the book's thick cover.

Wes opened his eyes. The boy was straddling him, but Wesley had survived the initial blow. He braced his feet against the boy's chest and pushed with all the strength his bony legs would allow. The stranger stumbled, and the gored book flew through the air, landing at Taylor's feet. She quickly scooped it up.

"Go, Tay! Go!!"

Taylor darted away. The boy grabbed at Wesley's ankle, but Wes used an outstretched hand to keep from falling. He righted himself then tore down the aisle after Tay, limbs flailing.

"Wait!" Taylor came to an abrupt halt. Wes nearly ran her over.

"What are you doing?!"

"Who is that kid?" she asked.

"I don't care!" Wesley couldn't believe they were having this conversation. "He tried to kill us! We need to get Ms. Easton. Now!"

"*Now* you want to tell?"

"Uhh... yeah?! He's got a knife!"

Taylor tossed the book to Wesley, the dagger's blade held firmly within its pages. "Not anymore," she said with a grin. She was smiling. *She was actually smiling!* Even worse, she'd turned around and was starting back toward the boy.

"Taylor? Tay!"

Wesley looked about and saw the tour had moved on without them. He shook his head and pulled the dagger from the book before starting after his friend.

Strangely, they found the stranger had retreated to a spot beneath a desk. His head snapped up as the kids tiptoed toward him. Tears were streaming down his cheeks.

Taylor was quick to put her hands into the air, palms out with nothing to hide.

"It's okay," she said. "I promise. We didn't mean to scare you. Alright? We aren't like that. We're friends. We aren't going to hurt you." Wesley kept his eyes on the boy as Taylor offered him a hand. "Why are you crying? Are you lost? You know, maybe we can help. Is there somewhere you're supposed to be?"

The stranger measured their intentions with innocent eyes before slowly moving to accept Taylor's help.

And then he answered.

CHAPTER 3

DOUGLAS CHECKED HIS watch before looking the room over. Ms. Easton was near the front with a group of kids gathered around her so she could explain the Dewey Decimal System. Hope was showing kids how to use the card catalogue to search for books. With the other adults busy, Douglas motioned his son over.

"Yeah?" Randy asked.

"Stay with the group," Douglas said. "I think Wesley and that girl fell behind. I'm gonna see if I can find them before they get themselves in trouble."

"They never get in trouble, but okay."

Douglas rubbed Randy's head then started down the corridor into the library's main hall. He stopped, looking about at the literature displays.

The now empty room was eerily quiet until Douglas heard excited voices just ahead.

"Now you wanna tell?" a young girl asked in a high pitched voice.

"Uhh...yeah?! He's got a knife!"

"Not anymore."

Douglas started toward the voices.

"Taylor? Tay!"

Douglas saw Wesley just as he disappeared around the corner. The boy had a book in one hand and – strangely, enough – a knife in the other. Surprisingly, Douglas did not pursue the children. Instead, he turned away, started toward the spiral staircase, and pulled a cell phone from his pocket. He dialed then put the phone to his ear.

"Tell him I'm upstairs and ready."

❖ ❖ ❖

Outside, the bus was parked in a new location across the street. But the dark town car that Wesley had noticed before was still sitting on the curb.

The driver hung up then turned to look at the shadowy figure in the backseat.

"Second floor," he said. "You're good to go."

The dark figure answered with a nod then faded away like smoke on the wind.

❖ ❖ ❖

Back in the library, the strange boy's answer was hanging in the air like a stubborn fog refusing to lift in the morning sun.

"Wait," Wesley said. "What did you say?"

"I need to speak with The Librarian."

"No... the other part..."

"I think Neverland's in danger."

"That's what I thought you said."

Taylor grabbed Wes by the arm and dragged him into a nearby corner. "This is crazy," she whispered. "What are we supposed to do?"

Wesley studied the odd boy. His clothes were a coarse weave, and he wore strange boots made from animal hide and tied with rough strips of leather. His hair was as wild and unkempt as a beaver dam. He certainly looked the part. *Peter Pan* was a tough read, but the Lost Boys were some of the most iconic and memorable characters in all of literature. If the Lost Boys were real, this was how they looked.

"I don't know, Tay. When you left, I... I saw something."

"Okay?"

"You'll think I'm nuts."

Taylor smirked, her look telling Wes to get on with it.

"It's hard to explain. There was this light and there was wind and I heard birds chirping. It was all coming out of that." Wesley stabbed a finger at the Neverland carving. Taylor stared at him blankly. "What?"

"You're right. I think you're nuts. Tell me how light can pass through a block of wood, especially when there's nothing but a brick wall on the other side."

Wesley groaned, dismissing Taylor with a wave of his hand. He stepped toward the stranger, but the boy quickly recoiled, moving aside so there was a chair between them.

Wesley stopped in his tracks. He'd forgotten he still had the knife in one hand and the speared book in the other. "No, no, no! I don't want to fight. Not again." He set both items down on a nearby desk. "See? I'm not going to hurt you." He looked away. "I probably couldn't if I tried."

Taylor covered her grin with a single hand. The boy was beginning to relax and took a reluctant step from behind the chair.

"What's your name?" Wesley asked.

"Locke."

"Locke? I'm Wesley. That's Taylor." She put a hand into the air but didn't wave. "You said you're from Neverland, right? Like... *the* Neverland?"

"Is there another Neverland?"

"Okay? But how did you get *here*?"

"Through the portal."

"The carving on the wall?"

Locke answered with a nod. Wesley looked over at Tay as two of the puzzle pieces rattling around in his skull clicked together.

"Can you show us?" he asked.

"I told you: I have to see The Librarian first."

"How do you know him? Most people have never seen the guy."

"He brought me here; offered to make me Neverland's Watcher."

"Wait a minute," Wesley said. "You're saying The Librarian has been to Neverland?"

"Wes," Taylor whined.

"If I find him," Locke began, "he can explain a lot better than I can."

The corner of Wesley's mouth curled into a small grin. "Then lead the way."

❖ ❖ ❖

The Lost Boy led Wesley and Taylor down a long corridor on the library's upper level. Both kids trailed behind Locke so their conversation would go unheard.

"You can't just use this as an excuse to go snooping around," Taylor said.

"Like I'm the first kid in Astoria who went looking for The Librarian."

"This is different. You think this kid's your golden ticket."

"You don't believe him, do you?"

"That he's a Lost Boy?"

"Shh!"

Taylor lowered her tone. "I can't believe you *do*. You won the science fair for crying out loud! You know? Science? Facts, figures... reality!"

"If you saw what I saw..."

Wesley let his voice trail off.

Locke was stopped near a large oil painting on the corridor's wall. Wes and Taylor shared a confused look as their new friend ran his fingers along the painting's edge as if searching for something hidden behind its golden frame.

"What are you doing?" Taylor asked.

"I think this is the right one," Locke explained. "But it's been so long." His fingers stopped along the bottom edge of the frame. Moments later, there was a loud click as something unlatched and sent the painting swinging open to reveal a hidden passage that led into darkness.

All three peered into the corridor. There was barely enough light to see the layered cobwebs that clung to the walls and carpeted the stone floor.

"So much for urban legends," Wesley said.

Locke stepped into the passage. The others followed.

"You sure you want to do this?" Taylor asked.

"*You* wanted to help him."

There were two lamps hanging just inside the entry, but they were dimmer versions of those in the library's main hall. They did little to battle the shadows moving in on the children with every step they took.

Eventually, the trio came to a junction that presented two long corridors and a ladder that seemed to disappear into a mist-filled cavern beneath their feet.

"Okay," Taylor began, "I'm not going down there. I don't care what anyone says. The spider webs *up here* are enough to make my skin crawl."

"Since when are you such a wuss?" Wesley asked.

"I don't like spiders. What? Sue me."

Locke sniffed the air. "This way."

The passage ahead of them was black as night and would be impossible to navigate without something to guide them. Luckily, there was a rusty lantern hanging from a large hook on the wall. Wesley reached for it, but Locke grabbed his arm and yanked him away.

"What?" Wesley asked defensively.

He followed Locke's upward gaze. While it was hard to make out in the darkness, there was a large boulder shaped like a teardrop floating in the air above them. The mammoth stone was hanging from a chain that twisted through an elaborate pulley system before disappearing into a hole in the wall.

"Booby trap," Locke explained matter-of-factly.

Wesley couldn't believe it. His trip to the library had started so terribly. Who would have guessed he'd be avoiding booby traps before the day was out? It was too cool. He quickly slung the backpack from his shoulder, fell to one knee, and pulled a hand-held video game from one of the zippered pockets. When Locke saw it, he snatched the game from Wesley's hand.

"Where'd you get this?" he asked, his tone demanding an answer.

"Umm... it was a present."

Locke studied it from every angle.

"What does it do?"

"It's for playing games. You wanna see?"

"It's not a weapon?"

Wesley shook his head, and Locke reluctantly handed the game back.

"I'm sorry," Locke said. "It's just... I've seen something like this before."

"In Neverland?"

Locke nodded. Wesley and Taylor shared a confused look.

Wes turned the game on and held it up in the air. The blue-green glow of its screen offered just enough light to ensure the three wouldn't run into a wall or blindly offer themselves up to some monster lurking beyond the light. Wesley held it ahead of them and led Taylor and Locke down the passage – past the point of no return.

❖ ❖ ❖

Ms. Easton was rapidly losing control of her class. A few students were lined up at the circulation desk to check out books with the library cards they'd been issued, but most were off somewhere doing their own thing. And they were being loud. They were being *very* loud.

"Guys! I need you to settle down! Please!"

No one looked up to acknowledge her. They were all having too much fun. She could handle the rowdy group in a classroom, but this was different. On a field trip, Ms. Easton needed help. That's what chaperones were for.

The teacher found Randy holding court in a corner with Caleb and a few others. She grabbed him by the arm and pulled him away from his friends.

"Oww! Ms. Easton! What'd I do?"

"Something, I'm sure. But right now, I'm looking for your dad."

Randy pointed toward the front of the building. "He went looking for Wesley and Taylor. If you wanna yell at anyone, yell at them."

"Will you find him, please? Thank you."

Randy gestured for Caleb to join him in his search of the library, but Ms. Easton stepped into Caleb's path before he had a chance to go anywhere.

"Randy doesn't need any help." She turned Caleb around so he was pointed in the opposite direction. "Why don't you find a book to check out like you're supposed to?"

Caleb groaned but did as he was told. Randy was about to do the same when Ms. Easton grabbed him by the arm again. She looked down her nose at the boy, this time using *her* tiny voice so no one else would hear. "Tell your dad it would be nice if he took his job a little more seriously. Just because you aren't much of a student doesn't mean he has to be a lousy chaperone."

❖ ❖ ❖

"There's something ahead," Wesley said. "See?"

"Really?" Taylor's voice was beginning to fray along with her nerves. "Where?" She craned her neck and saw two lights at the end of the shaft.

The kids came out of the darkness and into the dim glow of the newly discovered lamps. The lights were hanging on either side of a door that seemed to be the backside of a painting like the one they'd used to access the passage.

"I bet this leads right back into the library," Wesley said.

Tay batted her hair. "Are you serious? Please tell me we didn't go through this for nothing! I've got cobwebs all over me!"

"Really?" Wesley said in a mocking tone. "Did you break a nail?"

"Shut up!"

Wesley tucked his game into his pocket. He sensed Locke was apprehensive about something just as he'd been when he spotted the booby trap before.

"What's wrong?" he asked.

Locke's eyes were fixed on the painting, specifically two small holes that were cut side-by-side into the canvas. "Someone's in there," he said.

"The Librarian?"

"Someone else," Locke said in a low voice.

Wesley moved to a large block nearby. It was one of the dark stones used to build the library, an extra that had been cast aside. "Help me with this."

Locke hurried over, and the two boys struggled to push the stone across the ground one stubborn inch at a time.

"What are you doing?" Taylor asked.

"I just want to make sure," Wesley said.

"Make sure? Make sure *what*?"

"Tay, would you be quiet?!"

Wesley and Locke centered the stone in front of the painting. Wes stepped up onto the giant block. He shielded his eyes with both hands and peered through the spy holes into the next room.

Locke shivered as if a cold chill had run the length of his spine. He turned to face Tay. "They're here," Locke whispered. "I can feel it. You've got them, too."

Taylor saw Locke had removed his dagger from its sheath and had it at the ready. "Who?" she asked. "Who's here?"

"Pirates."

CHAPTER 4

A LARGE, FLOOR-TO-CEILING portrait of Mark Twain was hanging on a wall in The Librarian's study. It was an impressive piece despite the fact Twain's wise eyes had been replaced by those of a young child.

Wesley didn't have a full view of the room, but he got what he came for.

That's him? Wesley thought quietly to himself. *It's just a crusty old man!*

For Wes, this was his first opportunity to experience the dramatic tug-o-war between myth and reality. The kids in Astoria had spent years swapping stories about their library's reclusive caretaker. So many, in fact, that over time the legend grew so great that no one could have lived up to it – let alone the frail old man standing in the next room.

Stationed behind a large desk, The Librarian leaned heavily on a bone-colored cane. His hair was thick and silver, accented by an occasional stripe of black and combed away from his head like the quills on a porcupine. His clothes were custom-made from the finest fabrics and were quite regal: black pants, a dark purple vest, and a muted bowtie. He wore wire-framed spectacles that were perched at the end of a nose so thin and long it seemed cartoonish.

"What are you doing here?" The Librarian said in a hoarse voice.

Wesley flinched, sure he was caught until someone answered.

"You look surprised to see me."

Wesley leaned forward just in time to see Douglas Stanford step into view.

"Using your son's field trip as a way to sneak through the front door is beneath even you, Douglas. Besides, it's *him* I'm surprised to see." The old man motioned across the room. A lean man in a black cloak was studying the old books stacked in misshapen columns against the wall. "I suppose I shouldn't be. You read Irving's book until the pages fell out. Of course, that's when you were still rooting for the book's *protagonist*."

"I'm not that naïve, old man. Not anymore. I grew up, remember? The world isn't as black-and-white as your precious books make it out to be. You forget: everyone's the hero in their own story."

"And you forget: true heroes never give their own story much thought."

Douglas cracked a smile. "You think you can lecture me on selflessness?"

In the passage, Taylor was growing impatient. "Is it The Librarian?"

"I think," Wesley whispered. "But Randy's dad's in there, too."

The Librarian drew in a long breath. "Is that really why you're here? So we can rehash the past?"

"You know why I'm here," Douglas said.

"Do you think I've given up? I spend every night scouring my texts for the slightest change that might exist. I've established Watchers in each of the storybook lands. I'm doing everything I can. I will send you back. I just need–"

"More time? It's been thirty years! Do you have any idea what I've been through? Do you know what it's like to live some nightmarish version of your own life?"

"I can't imagine," The Librarian said solemnly.

"Even if you *could* send me back, it's too late for that now. I've built a life for myself *here*. I need a happy ending in *this world* – even if I have to write it myself."

The Librarian hung his head. "Then I'm afraid I can't help you, old friend."

"Fine," Douglas said. "But we've tried it your way. And I've heard all the apologies I can take." He stepped away. "Bones, see if you can convince this old teacher of mine to do the right thing and give us what we want."

There was something in Douglas's voice that reminded Wesley of the man's son. He felt like he was looking into a funhouse mirror that was reflecting some distorted version of his own life.

The Librarian straightened up as the hooded man turned away from the books. The dark figure loosened his glove one finger at a time then pulled it off to reveal a skeletal hand with skin so pale it seemed translucent. When he flexed his fingers into a fist, Wesley was sure one of the bony extremities would break through the impossibly thin skin.

Douglas turned away. "I don't even want to keep it. You can just pretend I checked it out like any other book on the shelf."

The Librarian's eyes darted back and forth between Douglas and the man in the black cloak. "Douglas, you're asking for something I cannot give. You must understand that? If you just give me—"

The hooded man shoved The Librarian into his chair then grabbed him, wrapping his long fingers around the old man's arm.

The Librarian cried in pain. Wesley winced, watching as the hooded man's hand began to glow. There was a flash of flame as The Librarian's sleeve caught fire. "Call him off! Douglas!"

"What's going on?" Taylor said loudly. "What was that?"

Wesley fired her a sharp look. "Quiet, Tay!"

"Stop telling me to—"

"Shut up!"

Wesley turned back to the painting, shielding his eyes once more to see—

The cloaked stranger was staring back at him, his eyes orange flames dancing beneath the darkness of his hood!

Wesley backed away from the painting. The color drained from his face. He fell from the stone and landed on his backside.

"What's wrong?" Taylor asked.

Before Wes could answer, a gloved fist tore through the painting from the other side. The hooded man ripped the canvas down the middle and exposed the children in the passage.

"Ruuun!"

Douglas pointed, barking an order: "Stop them!"

The cloaked figure tore what was left of the portrait from the wall. He tossed the heavy pieces aside and started after the children.

But The Librarian sprang into action.

Using the distraction to his advantage, The Librarian pushed Douglas aside and shoved his bony shoulder into his office bookcase. The bookcase toppled, catching the cloaked man by surprise and knocking him to the ground.

The old man bolted into the corridor as the kids began to scramble, finally shaking from their daze.

"Come," The Librarian said, ushering them down the passage. "You've put yourself in incredible danger."

Wesley looked down at the old man's arm. There was a hole in the sleeve of his silk shirt. It was singed at the edges and revealed pink skin where his arm had been burned so badly it was already beginning to blister.

"Are you okay?"

"There isn't time! We have to move. Now!"

The hooded man launched the heavy bookcase across the room with a single hand. Wesley looked back as they crossed into the darkness of the corridor. Douglas and the cloaked figure were stepping into the passage right behind them.

❖ ❖ ❖

"We're dead!" Taylor screeched. "Oh, man! We're dead! We're dead! We're *so* dead!" She was in the lead, scurrying down the passage with arms stretched out in front of her, one hand feeling along the brick wall as they went.

The ring of keys on Locke's belt produced a steady jingle with every step.

"What's that sound?! What's that sound?!"

"Keep going!" Wesley shouted. "We're almost there!"

The kids took a sharp right into the next passage. They knew their way from this point but slowed when they saw The Librarian stop near the old lantern hanging from the hook.

The old man faced them. "Who are you children? What are you... you're that boy from Neverland... the Watcher. What are you doing here?"

"The story's changed," Locke said. "Just like you said it might."

Lines of worry creased the old man's face. "Do the others know?"

"Hook says he's met someone from the real world. That's all I know."

The Librarian looked down the passage as if the answer to everything was right behind them. "What is happening here?"

The shuffle of footsteps echoed down the shaft.

"Go! Find someplace to hide!" The Librarian ordered.

"But—"

"Go!" The old man's booming voice seemed to come from somewhere deep within him, a place hidden and ancient. "Go now!"

Wesley looked down the corridor. A pair of orange eyes were bouncing around in the darkness as the hooded man approached.

The kids took off. The Librarian waited for them to round the corner then rested his hand on the hanging lantern.

Those flaming eyes were closing in. Dancing in the dark. Closer. And closer. Until eventually The Librarian's pursuers were stepping into the lantern's light.

Douglas stopped and cast a satisfied glare at The Librarian. The hooded man stepped forward, and The Librarian pulled the lantern from the wall.

Suddenly, chains and moving gears rattled from inside the passage walls. The smirk vanished from Douglas's face. "Wait!" he shouted. He looked up just in time to see the boulder begin its descent. Both men leapt aside to avoid the boulder, but the falling stone was never meant for them. It was merely the catalyst needed to activate the trap. Instead, a thick set of cobwebs pulled free from the stone floor and quickly scooped the two up, pulling Douglas and the hooded man toward the ceiling.

The Librarian watched the netting sway back-and-forth, his attackers trapped some twelve feet over his head. But even from his new position, Douglas was still trying to win. He reached through the sticky netting as The Librarian moved toward a ladder that led into the caverns beneath the library. "Go ahead and run, you old fool! It's better that way!" Douglas gritted his teeth. "Winning will taste so much better that way!"

CHAPTER 5

THE OIL PAINTING swung open, and the children tumbled out, landing in a pile of arms and legs just outside the passage. Locke was quick to his feet while Wesley and Taylor struggled to recover.

"What the heck is going on?" Taylor asked. "What was that thing?"

"You believe he's from Neverland now?"

"You're seriously stopping to say 'I told you so?'"

Wesley looked about. "We've gotta find Ms. Easton."

"What's she gonna do?"

He shot her a look. Tay was right. This was a bit outside their teacher's area of expertise. "Then what do we do?"

"Two options," Locke explained. "We fight... or we hide."

The kids looked to one another then emphatically answered in unison. "We hide!"

"And if they find us?"

Wesley gave this a moment's thought. "We make sure they don't. C'mon!"

Wes led the others down the stone staircase and into the library's main hall. They didn't question him. In that moment there was something about Wesley, an air of confidence he was wearing that didn't quite fit but made them want to follow all the same.

They snaked their way through the exhibits then sprinted down one of the long aisles. Wesley came to a halt, his sneakers squeaking on the tile floor as he gestured toward the giant woodcarvings that lined the wall.

"Pick," he said.

Taylor looked confused. "What?"

"If every one of these leads to another world—"

"No way, Wes! No!"

"Can you think of a better place to hide? Locke's right. What are we gonna do? Hide under the desk? If that thing finds us we're dead! Maybe Locke can take us to Neverland or—"

Locke's eyes brightened with excitement. "Or we can go someplace else!"

The Lost Boy quickly studied the Oz carving before them then hurried back up the aisle. He slid into the main hall, his eyes darting around until they found the *Wizard of Oz* display just a few feet away. The diorama had a number of items that were easily identifiable to anyone who knew the *Oz* story well: silver slippers, an oil can, three yellow bricks, and a thick, leather-bound book sitting open on a small podium alongside a magic wand that seemed to glow in the light. Locke grabbed the wand and hurried to rejoin his new friends.

Wesley and Taylor stepped aside so Locke could go to work. The Lost Boy's fingers searched the wooden landscape and discovered the dark tree in the forest shaped like the wand in his hand.

"Wes, we're wasting time. Those guys are gonna be out here any minute."

"Just watch," Wesley said.

Locke lined the wand up with the carving's dark imperfection then gently pushed it into place like the final piece of a strange jigsaw puzzle.

At first, the changes to the carving were subtle. The wood began to lighten in color, something few would have noticed if they weren't familiar with the strange piece. But soon, as the wood continued to change, the features of the carving began to fade until there was nothing in their place but a vivid pool of light.

Taylor stared in utter disbelief. "Oh my god!"

"See?" Wesley said. "See? What'd I tell you?"

Long tentacles of light began to extend from the pool's surface, coiling around the three children like the wispy fingers of a ghost.

"What's happening?" Taylor asked nervously.

"I don't know," Wesley giggled.

The light began to shimmer and ripple. Each tiny wave left a translucent patch in its wake. The patches were gone almost as quickly as they appeared, but Wesley could tell there was an old room with wooden walls waiting beyond the portal of light.

"W-Wesley?" Taylor whispered. "P-please."

It wasn't what she said, it was how she said it that finally got him. Their eyes met, and Wesley took her trembling hand. "It'll be okay," he said. "I promise."

Both turned their attention back to the carving. Its light was so intense they had to close their eyes and look away. But from that point forward neither let go of the other – not even when the wind began to howl, not even when the tentacles tightened and pulled them through the portal to the other side.

❖ ❖ ❖

"Get me down from this thing," Douglas snarled.

Without a word, the cloaked henchman obeyed. His body turned to grey smoke then streamed to the floor where it assumed its original form, that of a man, this time with a thin, crescent-shaped sword in hand.

The dark man drew his sword back and came down on the trap's sticky webs in a violent arc. Douglas readied himself for impact as the razor-sharp blade released him from the trap and sent him crashing to the floor.

As Douglas struggled to free himself from the netting, the hooded man was already moving toward the ladder The Librarian descended just a few moments before.

"Wait!" Douglas said. He came to his feet. "That's just what the decrepit old fool wants. He'll own us down there." He was talking though his teeth as he started down the corridor. "We're going after the kids."

❖ ❖ ❖

Wesley opened his eyes just in time to watch the small sphere of light floating in the air ahead of them wink out and disappear.

The kids were standing inside a wooden shack no bigger than a large shed. The floorboards creaked beneath their feet. The roof was leaky and sagged like it might collapse on their heads. In one corner, a pile of dead leaves had been pushed together alongside a collection of forgotten fruit that had shriveled with age.

Wesley and Taylor looked at one another then slowly dropped their gaze to their interlocked hands. Their eyes came up together. Each fired the other an accusing look before pulling away in embarrassment.

Wesley joined Locke near a dirty window across the room.

Taylor spun around. "Did it work? Because something about this doesn't seem right. How're we supposed to get back?"

The window was so filthy with dirt and muck Wesley had to clear a spot with his hand. "Whoa!" he whispered, his eyes filled with wonder after seeing what was waiting just beyond the glass. He and Locke started for the door, both with an extra zip of excitement in their step.

"Wes?" Taylor continued. "Where are you going? We have to—"

"In a minute!" Wesley followed Locke through the door. "You have to see this!"

Taylor cast one final glance around the cabin. Her eyes spied a metal oil can that was sitting on a tiny shelf on the opposite wall.

"Tay!" Wesley hollered. "Get out here!"

She shook her head in frustration then slowly walked through the door after them. She didn't make it far, though. None of them did. All three were glued to the spot when they saw the incredible vista that lay before them.

The cabin was nestled in a magnificent flower garden near the base of a small hill. Beyond that, a lush, green meadow unfolded into the distance. The meadow was bordered by a deep forest on one side and a towering waterfall that tumbled over a rocky cliff on the other. There was a narrow road woven through the landscape. Its yellow bricks caught the sunlight and formed a golden ribbon that led toward a city skyline on the horizon. Like giant prisms, the glass buildings captured the sun and sent it back into the world in brilliant, emerald-colored rays.

"Guys," Wesley began with a smile, "I don't think we're in Kansas anymore!"

CHAPTER 6

WESLEY WATCHED TAYLOR skip down the yellow brick road, elated.

"Oh my god! This is incredible!" She wheeled around with nothing but a toothy grin for her friends. "C'mon! Where do you wanna go first?"

Locke spoke before Wesley had a chance to answer. "Nowhere," he said. "We have to stay right where we're at. We—"

"Are you kidding me? Emerald City's right there!" Taylor pointed toward the city skyline that was taunting her from the horizon. "Who knows who we might meet on the way?"

Locke took a step toward her. "We can play and explore, but we're forbidden to interact with any of the people in this land."

Taylor looked at Locke, the wonder gone from her eyes. "Says who?"

"The rules."

Taylor playfully waved him off and sprinted into the meadow, arms extended on either side like the wings of an airplane. "Rules don't make sense in a place like this!"

Wesley used a cupped hand to help his voice carry. "I thought you were worried about getting back," he yelled.

"Back?" Taylor giggled. "Back where?"

Wesley watched, happy for his friend as she slowed to approach a pair of giant butterflies walking about in the grass. The size of a small car, they looked like something from one of the old Japanese horror movies his dad liked to watch on Sunday afternoons. For a moment, Wesley worried one of the mammoth insects might grab his friend and fly away with her. He wondered what he would do if that happened but didn't let his dark thoughts ruin the moment. He was enjoying Taylor's delight just a little too much for that.

Taylor tiptoed toward the butterflies, but they sensed her presence and took to the air with a quick flutter of their brightly-colored wings. "Hey!"

Taylor ran after them, her laughter loud and ever-present.

"Tay! We can't go too far! We still don't know how to get back!"

The butterflies seemed just as curious about Taylor as she was of them. They were circling her at a safe height – just barely out of reach. Taylor saw they weren't going far and froze, raising a hand into the air with a single finger extended.

"Taylor?" Wesley hollered.

She didn't answer. She stood like a statue, waiting for the butterflies to make the next move. And one of them finally did, gently landing on the perch her finger was there to provide.

Wesley ran into the meadow after his friend. "Oh, man! Wait for me!"

❖ ❖ ❖

Douglas pushed the painting open with little regard, letting the fine piece slam into the brick wall as he barged through the passage exit and into the library. He marched down the corridor and stopped near the railing that looked down into the main hall. "Randall!"

Randy appeared from one of the aisles. Looking up at Douglas, Randy seemed shaken by the tone of his father's voice.

"Did that Wesley kid come running through down there?"

"I didn't see him," Randy said. "Why?"

"Does it matter?"

Randy flinched. "N-no, sir."

"Yell if you see him. I don't want him or his friend getting out that door."

"Everyone is lining up out back. I think we're getting ready to leave. And Ms. Easton—"

"You let me worry about Ms. Easton."

"O-okay."

Douglas turned away from the railing. The hooded man had made sure to stand a few feet behind him so that he remained unseen.

"Find them," Douglas said in a voice that fit their surroundings. "We get those kids, and the old man will come looking for us. I promise."

The dark figure started back down the corridor, his cloak whipping in the air behind him. Douglas returned to the railing and looked down on his son once more. With a book in hand, Randy had already taken a seat on the floor near the lobby doors. He'd be there if Wesley and Taylor tried to escape. And he'd stop them. He'd stop them for his dad.

He was such a good boy.

❖ ❖ ❖

Locke and Taylor stood near the forest tree line, both with their eyes fixed on Wesley in one of the trees above them. He was standing nervously on a large branch about twenty feet overhead and gripping a thick vine that was clinging to one of the boughs above them.

"Either do it or climb down," Taylor hollered. "We're wasting time!"

Wesley put his foot into the air, ready to step off the limb only to immediately grab hold of the tree's massive trunk. He couldn't help himself. It was just a reflex reaction, like that time he kicked Dr. Travis when she hit him on the knee with her little, metal hammer.

"C'mon, Wes!"

"Yes," a grumpy voice said from behind him. "Listen to your friend, Wes."

Wesley turned just in time to see the trunk's bark pull away from the tree to reveal two eyes hiding in the tree's flesh. Eyes in the tree. They looked human. A mouth with sharp teeth and wooden lips appeared beneath the eyes. It was filled with wet muck that came alive with the worms crawling through it.

"Do it!" the mouth snarled, its lips grinding against tree bark as they moved. "Get out of my branches!"

Wesley tightened his grip and wrapped one leg around the vine before closing his eyes and stepping off the branch. He slid down the vine, falling fast and out-of-control until he could wrap his other leg around the vine to stabilize his descent. His feet hit the ground, and while his knees nearly gave out on him, he landed clean.

Taylor ran to his side, clapping. "Nice!"

"I know, right? Like it was my job. Nothing to it." Wesley looked around. "Where's Locke?"

"I... I don't know. Crazy little dude was right here a second ago."

They searched together. Then a handful of leaves floated down on them from above, and Wesley shifted his gaze upward.

"Hey!" Wesley yelled.

Locke was scaling the tree with one of the tree's vines held firmly between his teeth. He was moving quickly too, hand-over-hand, already well above the limb where Wesley had stopped.

"He needs to get down," Wesley explained.

"Why?" Taylor asked. "Worried he's gonna show you up?"

"We're in Oz, Taylor. That tree talked to me."

"What?"

"The tree talked to me!"

Taylor looked up at Locke just as he reached the tree's peak. He stepped onto the bough, both arms out for balance. Once steadied, a mischievous grin crept onto his face. Then, all at once, vine in hand, Locke sprinted the length of the branch and sprang into the air.

Taylor covered her mouth with a single hand. "Oh my god!"

"Akkkhhaaaaa!"

Locke's battle cry was loud and proud and carried beyond the meadow into the far reaches of Oz. His hair whipped in the air as he sailed head first toward the ground, the vine spiraling behind him like a corkscrew in his wake.

Wesley stood in awe, but Taylor watched in horror, no doubt convinced Locke was seconds from certain death. But the vine pulled taught and the change in momentum snapped Locke's small body around, swinging his legs to the front so he was no longer falling face first toward the ground. His legs thrashed wildly. The vine pulled him from his death spiral and allowed for a shallow landing. He crashed to earth, somersaulting through the grass before he came to rest, his arms and legs all pointing in seemingly impossible directions.

Wesley and Tay hurried over. Locke got to his feet and dusted himself off.

"Are you crazy?" Taylor screamed, her anger mingled with excitement. "Why'd you do that?"

"Because I *can*."

"That was the coolest thing I've ever seen!" she exclaimed.

Wesley noticed pink rushing into Taylor's cheeks and suddenly felt like calling Locke a show-off but bit his tongue.

Taylor started away, motioning for the boys to follow. "Now, c'mon. Let's get out of here before that thing starts throwing apples at us."

Confused, Locke looked back at the tree then turned to chase Taylor down.

Wesley watched them leave. Most days, Wes did everything he could to go unnoticed. Kids can't pick on you if they don't know you're there. Being with Taylor was an exception, though. It was the only time he didn't feel like he needed to disappear. Sometimes though, he found himself fading into the background anyway because she had so many friends. It rarely lasted. She was Wesley's best friend and never forgot to include him. And yet, for some reason, he worried she might today.

"Good job, Wes."

Wesley turned. The face in the tree's trunk had reappeared near its massive base. It didn't seem nearly as horrifying as it had before.

"Umm... yeah... thanks!"

Wesley took off and the strange being disappeared into the tree's trunk again.

He caught up to Locke who was already trailing a good distance behind Taylor. "Hey, man."

"Hey," Locke echoed.

"You think those guys will find us?"

"I doubt it. They might wait for us, but we won't be surprised this time. We'll be ready."

"I bet you fight guys like that all the time in Neverland, huh?"

"Every day."

Wesley took a spot beside Locke so they were walking side-by-side as they talked. He had something more to say but was trying to find the right words. "I'm sorry for what happened in the library. When we met. It's just... it happened so fast. I didn't have time to think."

"You were protecting your girl," Locke said. "I should say sorry to you."

"She's not my girl." Wesley cringed. That hadn't come out right. He quickly changed the subject. "So, I don't get it. If Neverland's *half* this cool, why would you ever waste time hanging out in a dead-end town like Astoria?"

"I only came to report what I saw."

"Oh," Wesley said. "That makes sense."

"What do you mean?"

"I can't imagine why you would come to our world if you didn't have to."

"Why not?"

"I moved to Astoria last year, and I read books just so I can get away from that place. You get fairies and Indian chiefs, pirates. We get... gym class." Wesley pointed to the tree they climbed. It was just about to disappear beneath the horizon. "That? I could never do something like that where I come from."

"You don't have trees in your world?"

"No. No, man. You don't understand. It's not about trees. It's my life." Wesley sighed. "My life... sucks."

"Life's what you make it, Wes."

Wesley chuckled. Locke was so naïve about the real world. Not that he held it against the kid. How could he know what middle school life was like for a boy like Wesley? How could he know Wesley spent more lunches hiding in the boy's bathroom than eating in the cafeteria?

"Maybe in Neverland. But sixth grade is a little more complicated than that. There's... drama." He shook his head. "I wear glasses. What do you think that means?"

"My friend wears glasses. We call him Goggles. He's in charge of the maps."

"Well, in my world they make me a geek. I don't get to be in charge of anything."

"Oh," Locke said quietly. "What's a geek?"

"Exactly!" Wesley said. "See? In my world there's all this stuff that matters to people. Do you have glasses? Are you athletic? What kind of clothes do you wear? Is it my fault my mom tries to dress me like I'm getting ready for the senior tour?" Locke didn't answer. "My life sucks, man. And the worst part? There's nothing I could have done about it. All that stuff kids think is so important, it's all stuff that's completely out of your control."

Wesley looked over to get Locke's response only to find the Lost Boy was no longer at his side. He had stopped a few feet back and was wearing an expression of absolute disgust.

"What?" Wesley asked. "What'd I say?"

"There isn't anyone in Neverland who wouldn't trade places with you."

Just ahead of them Taylor found a small grove of trees bearing silver lunch pails instead of fruit. When she turned to find the boys she saw they had stopped and were squared-off against one another. She rolled her eyes then headed their way.

"They don't know me, Locke. They don't know my life. Okay? Not to be a jerk, but *you* don't know me either." Wesley tried to keep his cool but really took issue with what Locke said. "I get bullied every day. Every day. Sound like fun? Your friends are really going to trade swimming with mermaids for that?"

"And what did you do *today* to make sure it doesn't happen *tomorrow*?"

"Easy for you to say. You're a freakin' Lost Boy."

"Who saved us back in the library?"

"I didn't save anyone. I had an idea. That's it. That's all I did. I said, 'let's go this way.' Doesn't make me a hero, does it? I'm just really good at running away."

Taylor arrived just as the boys were starting to talk over one another. "What's going on?"

Wesley motioned toward Locke. "Your new friend's trying to tell me that *Peter Pan* would rather be *Wesley Bates*. I guess he'd rather be Astoria's *biggest loser* than Neverland's *biggest hero*, huh, Locke?"

"Don't say that about yourself! You're not–"

Taylor came to an abrupt halt when Locke stormed away.

Wesley shook his head. "Why're *you* mad? At least she's my friend. I just met you, and you're already telling me how to live my life."

The Lost Boy stopped, looking back. "I think you're yelling at the wrong people. My friends, everyone in Neverland, they have to live the life someone wrote for them. It never changes. It's the same, every single day."

"Really? Then why can *you* do anything you want?"

Locke stepped toward him. While Wesley fumed, Locke was in complete control, his movements perfectly measured, each of his words carefully chosen to hammer his point home. "Have you read *Peter Pan*?"

"Twice," Wesley answered smugly.

"And have you heard of Locke Underfoot?"

"Never!"

"*That's* why."

Locke's final words came in a hushed tone, but Wesley heard the sorrow hiding behind his soft breath. He'd forced Locke to open up about his own issues and felt bad about it as Locke turned to leave once more.

"Locke? I'm sorry. I just—"

The Lost Boy stopped again. This time he refused to look Wesley in the eye. "Do you even know why you're apologizing?"

Wesley didn't answer.

"You know what's great about your world?" Locke rattled the keys on his belt. "Because maybe one day I won't have the right key. It's real life, not some fairy tale written to put kids to bed at night."

That one made Taylor wince.

"You get bullied, Wes? I have to watch a friend drink the same bottle of poison over and over again, all because it's written in some stupid book." He blew out a disgusted breath. "Her life is controlled by words on a page. You've got a chance to write your own story... and you don't."

CHAPTER 7

TAYLOR AND LOCKE sat together in the meadow, both eating from silver lunch pails they'd picked from a nearby tree. Wesley was with them but sat alone, perched on a hollow log near the tree line with a bottle of water at his feet, his open backpack on the ground beside that. While his friends marveled at a towering mountain range in the distance, Wesley's thoughts were even further away. He was still hurting after the argument with Locke. Not that Locke had said anything particularly mean-spirited. Truthfully, he wished Locke had. Randy had said worse, and it had never taken Wesley this long to recover. But Locke had echoed what people had been telling him all year, and it hurt.

Stand up for yourself, Wes.

Life's what you make it.

Believe in yourself.

Stop hiding who you are.

It was like the script for a lame after-school special. Wesley was sick of it. Everyone Wesley knew had been singing from the same hymn book, but now this kid from Neverland was chiming in too. It was too much. His dad had a question he liked to ask. "What's more likely," he'd say, "that you're right, and everyone's wrong – or maybe it's the other way around?" Wesley was glad his dad wasn't there to ask him that now.

Taylor stood up with her pail in hand. "What do we do when we're done?"

"I don't know," Locke said. He rubbed his hands together as he came to his feet. "This is a new one for me, too."

Wesley watched Locke take the pail from Taylor before raising up onto his tip-toes so he could hang it on one of the tree branches. Almost immediately, he wished he had done it for her instead.

Locke was sniffing the air again when Wesley and Taylor went to hang the other pails. His nose led him deeper into the woods until he found a narrow path that wound its way through the trees.

Taylor came to his side. "How do you do that?"

Wesley followed them down the path, keeping a close watch on the trees as they moved deeper into the forest. None were coming alive like the one he'd climbed before, but they seemed to change as the kids traveled. Each was a little more barren than the last, until eventually they were in an area of the forest where the trees didn't have any leaves at all. Instead, their gnarled branches twisted into bony hands that reached for the sky.

Wesley quickened his pace and caught up with his friends.

The children let Locke lead the way until they crested a hill that looked down on a small stone cottage in the distance. A ribbon of smoke curled from its brick chimney and escaped into the pale blue sky.

"Oh man!" Wesley exclaimed. "Look!"

The others followed Wesley's gaze until their attention landed on a young girl who was chopping wood near the cottage below.

Of course, she wasn't a girl. Not really.

They were in Oz.

She was a Munchkin.

❖ ❖ ❖

Back in the library, the hooded man lifted a table with one hand, tipping it on edge to make sure no one was hiding beneath it before letting the table crash to the floor.

His cloak billowed as he turned to a nearby desk and kicked it over. He seemed to be growing irater with every moment that passed. If only he had slowed his angry search, perhaps he would have noticed the shadow looming behind a grate on the wall – or the old man who was casting it while he watched the thug's every move.

❖ ❖ ❖

"I can't believe we're doing this," Taylor whispered as she and the others sneaked to a hiding spot behind a small well on the outermost edge of the cottage owner's land.

The Munchkin girl was short and squat and wore faded overalls. Her skin was colored a soft pink and seemed to reflect the sunlight like the skin of a porcelain doll. She was covered in mud and had accomplished little since starting her work. Her axe was as big as she was, and the pile of logs that needed chopping was a mountain compared to the neatly stacked firewood she'd produced so far.

The kids watched as the Munchkin maiden studied her hands. Her skin was cracked, her fingers worn red and bleeding.

"We should help," Taylor whispered.

"We can't," Locke said.

"I know, but she's so—"

Someone cut Tay off before she could finish.

"What's taking so long, child?!" It was a tiny voice, but an angry one that forced the kids to pull together behind the well for cover.

Afraid herself, the maiden struggled to lift her axe as an ugly old woman came out of the cottage and marched toward her.

"Such a waste of space," she snarled. "I swear!"

"I'm trying my best, ma'am. I promise I'll—"

"Don't whine to me, little girl! If your loving woodsman had never disappeared on us you wouldn't have so much to do, now would you?"

Wes saw a spark of recognition in Taylor's eyes. She was moving to get a better look, but Locke was quick to hold her back.

The old woman threw up her arms in disgust. "I guess you want another night without supper! Is that it?"

"Please, no!"

"It won't worry me any if you fade away to nothing. Your lover certainly did!" The ugly woman stormed away toward the cottage. "I want that wood split and stacked by nightfall. And don't forget you've got chores in the house when you're finished here!"

The maiden watched until her mistress was up the stairs and in the house then let out a long, tired sigh. Her eyes fell on the chopping block in front of her where a single log stood at attention. She gathered her strength and lifted the axe, but the tool's weight sent the maiden toppling backwards into the mud. She landed hard and sat in the muck for a long moment before she broke down and began to sob.

Behind the well, Taylor turned to face Wesley. "You know who that is?"

"Yeah. It's the Tin Man's girlfriend."

"It's not his girlfriend, Wes." Tay was upset he'd phrased it that way. "She's his fiancée. She's his soulmate."

"Who's the Tin Man?" Locke interrupted.

"You've never seen..."

Taylor's words trailed off. Of course Locke had never seen the movie she and Wesley knew so well. He didn't know anything about *The Wizard of Oz*. It was just another carving on the library wall, a doorway into a world he'd never visited until now.

The children snuck away. Locke listened as his new friends took turns telling the Tin Man's story.

"The Tin Man is from a story called *The Wizard of Oz*. He's – well, he's a man made of metal."

"Right," Taylor said. "Only he wasn't always made of metal. In the beginning... he was just a man."

"The Woodsman was in love with the Munchkin maiden. She promised to marry him as soon as he could afford to give them a proper home."

"Only things weren't easy for them. The Woodsman was very poor–"

"And she lived with an evil old woman who treated the maiden like a slave and forced the maiden to wait on her hand-and-foot."

"The Woodsman promised the maiden he'd work hard and earn enough so he could come back and give her the life she deserved."

"But the old woman wasn't going to let the maiden go that easy."

"Exactly," Taylor said. "The old woman went to the Wicked Witch of the East, and—"

"Witch?" Locke asked, interrupting.

"There are witches in Oz," Taylor explained. "Some are good, some are bad. She's one of the worst."

"She promised the witch two sheep and a cow if she would keep the marriage from happening."

"The witch agreed."

"That night the witch cast a spell on the Woodsman's axe. The next day the axe leapt from his hand, sailed through the air, and cut off one of his legs."

"Oh my gosh!" Locke was shocked the story had taken such a dramatic turn.

"The witch was convinced that would be good enough," Taylor continued.

"Really," Wesley said. "Who's going to cut wood on one leg?"

"The Woodsman," Taylor said. "That's who."

"He'd do anything to keep his promise so he found a tinsmith who was good enough to make him a leg out of tin. It was stronger than his real leg, and in a few days he was cutting wood better than ever."

"Then what happened?" Locke asked, somewhat hesitant.

"Every time he stepped foot into the forest his axe would take another limb. One after another. His legs. His arms. Until eventually, there was nothing left to take at all."

Taylor frowned. "Even then, though. Even as he began to realize he was fighting a losing battle. All he could think about was her."

"He went back to work, but the axe jumped from his hands once more and finally split the Woodsman's body in two."

"The tinsmith worked through the night, but there was little he could do. He pieced the Woodsman together but couldn't rebuild what mattered most to the Woodsman: his heart."

"The Woodsman was beaten. He didn't think the Munchkin maiden would love a man without a heart so he disappeared into the forest. She never saw him again."

Wesley and Taylor led Locke out of the forest and into the meadow. Both knew he would have questions and waited patiently.

"Why would someone write that?" Locke asked. "Your heart doesn't have anything to do with love."

"That's what makes it so sad," Wesley said.

"So sad."

The three walked in silence until the cabin re-appeared on the horizon and planted an idea in Taylor's mind. "Maybe it doesn't have to be," she suggested.

"What do you mean?" Wesley asked.

"Who says we can't find him for her?"

"Whoa! Wait a minute, now. We can't–"

Taylor cut Wesley off. "What if that's his house? I saw an oil can on the shelf. That would mean he's close, right?"

"We can't, Tay. You know that."

"Why?"

"Because Locke said it's against the rules!"

"Yeah? But why? Who came up with these rules anyway?"

Both turned to Locke who didn't seem ready to join their conversation.

"It's like we're in a time-travel movie." Wesley fell to one knee and picked a pink flower from the grass. "Even picking this flower can change the way things are supposed to happen." He moved his focus from Taylor to Locke. "That's what you're supposed to watch for, right? Changes in the story?"

The Lost Boy nodded.

"But we helped Locke," Taylor explained. "If *that* was right, how can *this* be wrong?"

The three children stood facing one another in silence until Locke finally spoke up. "Are they important to the story or are they just... in the background... like me?"

Taylor shrugged. "The Munchkin maiden is barely mentioned. I think she shows up on one or two pages, that's it. Most people don't even know she's part of the story."

She and Locke looked to Wesley, as if his was the deciding vote.

"Is this what you were talking about?" Wesley asked. "Being trapped in a story?"

Locke pointed back in the direction from which they'd come. "That girl will wake up to the same pile of wood every morning. It will never change. She'll be working for that old lady forever. Not the rest of her life. Forever. 'Til the world ends."

"It's a chance to give them a happy ending, Wes."

Wesley shook his head, finally giving in.

"Fine," he said in a huff. Taylor jumped into the air, giddy with excitement. "What's the worst that can happen anyway?"

CHAPTER 8

THE CHILDREN KNEW their chances of finding the Tin Man were slim. They were short on time, and the forest seemed to go on forever in all directions. He could be anywhere. But then—

Wesley stopped and put a balled fist into the air. "Did you hear that? Listen!"

Taylor and Locke were at a distance on either side of him. They'd made sure to stay within sight of one another, but they were spread out in an effort to cover as much ground as possible in their search. Taylor listened, but all she heard was the bubbling of a nearby brook.

"Hmph!"

"There!" Wesley said. "This way!"

Wesley took off. Taylor and Locke quickly followed.

Wesley came into a small clearing but tripped and fell face first into the dirt. He rolled onto his side, looking back to see his foot was hooked on a grey tree stump jutting out from the ground. There was another stump beside that one and another beside that.

"Tell me you guys didn't see that," Wesley joked.

Taylor and Locke had just stepped into the clearing behind him, but neither answered. Both were staring at something directly behind Wesley.

"Wes?" Taylor whispered.

"Hmph!"

Wesley rolled onto the flat of his stomach. Someone was towering over him from just a few feet away. While the sun was in his eyes, Wes could see the stranger was holding a large axe and was ready to bring it down on his head.

"No! Don't!" Wesley pulled his knees into his chest and covered his head with both arms, bracing for the impact of the stranger's axe. When it didn't come, Wesley poked his head back into the open.

The stranger hadn't moved an inch. Wesley raised a hand to shield his eyes from the light. The man wasn't ready to bring the axe down on Wesley like the boy had thought. Instead, he was holding it mid-swing, ready to send it into the half-chopped tree that stood before him. He was frozen in time, his joints rusted. The man was made of tin.

❖ ❖ ❖

Locke sprinted through the woods, his keys jangling, an oil can gripped tightly in his left hand.

"I can't believe we actually found him," Wesley said. He and Taylor stood together in the clearing. "This forest is so big. You know how lucky we got?"

"It's like it was meant to be," Taylor said.

"Hmph!" The Tin Man sounded like an old man whose grandchildren had glued his lips together as a prank.

"Hold on," Taylor said. "We're here to help."

Both kids turned when Locke appeared in the clearing. Locke handed the oil can to Tay. "You really think this is going to work?" he asked.

"There's only one way to find out." Taylor took the cap from the oil can's spout and began to grease the hinged joint in the Tin Man's leg.

❖ ❖ ❖

Randy was still at his post near the lobby doors. He was flipping through the mammoth volume he'd taken from the shelf: a gorgeous printing of Taylor's favorite book, *The Wizard of Oz*. Surprisingly, Randy had grown to appreciate the beautiful illustrations that were scattered throughout the tome and the fine craftsmanship that had gone into its production. He was enjoying the story, too. Randy wasn't much of a reader, but the book was a nice departure from what had been a pretty crummy day. Field trips were supposed to be fun, but so far his dad had yelled at him and Ms. Easton had treated him like some kind of criminal. The day wasn't going exactly as he had planned.

But Randy was five chapters into the story when something unfathomable happened that made him forget all of that. He gasped as words in the book began to break apart, floating across the page like the noodles in an alphabet soup. His hands shook. Beads of sweat formed on his upper lip. He saw the same thing every time he thumbed to a new page: nothing but a swirling whirlpool of black ink where the story should have been.

Then, all around him, the building began to tremble and Randy's mind quickly shifted gears. He tossed the book to the floor. The ground rocked. He struggled to keep his balance as dust rained down from the ceiling.

"Dad!"

Douglas hurried down the staircase. The building's waver was becoming more violent with each passing moment. Books fell from shelves. Desk drawers rattled open. A lamp clattered across a nearby desk. It was like the library was crumbling, ready to come down all around them. Douglas ran for his son, grabbing the young boy's arm and pulling him under a long table for cover.

❖ ❖ ❖

Back in Oz, Taylor worked to grease each of the Tin Man's joints. Whenever she squirted a dollop of oil, the Tin Man moaned as if it gave him great relief. Occasionally, he tested his newfound mobility as she moved onto another of his locked joints. When she was finally finished, Tay and her friends stepped back to watch as the Tin Man took his first awkward steps since being caught in the rain.

"My goodness," he said in a high voice. "Thank you so very much." He reached for the sky to see just how much freedom the kids had given him. "I've been holding that axe for more than a year. It is a great comfort to be free. I might have stood there for always if you hadn't come along. How did you happen to find me?"

Wesley and Taylor looked at one another, neither sure how to respond. When Locke didn't step in, it was Taylor who finally answered.

"We were looking for you."

"Looking for me?" The Tin Man's voice had a funny echo to it. Every word seemed to hang around just a little longer than it should. "Why would you be looking for me?"

Taylor stepped toward him. "We're here to help you get back to your fiancée."

The Tin Man stared at her blankly then looked away. "I don't have a fiancée."

He grabbed his axe.

"What?" Wesley asked.

The Tin Man was walking away from them, ready to disappear into the woods. "You say you're my friends, but I can see you are from a place far away from here." The kids had to follow to keep from losing him. "Monsters like me don't get happy endings in the Land of Oz."

"Don't say that about yourself," Taylor said. "Don't you dare say that."

Wesley smirked. This was starting to sound a bit familiar.

"Could you love a man without a heart?" the Tin Man asked.

"Does that stop you from loving her?"

This finally gave the Tinman pause.

"Then why would it matter to her?"

The Tin Man began to pace.

"You don't have to see her," Wesley explained. "If you don't want to—"

"He *wants* to, Wes."

"Maybe he doesn't."

The Tin Man hung his head. "I've thought of nothing else for all the time my joints have been frozen. But now that I'm free..." He spoke in a whisper that trailed off into nothing at the end. He didn't have to finish. Wesley suddenly understood the Tin Man better than he ever had when reading the ratty copy of *Oz* that was buried in his closet. Yes, sir. It was all starting to feel very familiar now.

"You're afraid," Wesley said quietly.

The Tin Man turned to face Wesley. He forced a stiff shrug. "What if she runs the moment she sees me? What if she's found someone else?"

"What if she hasn't?" Wesley suggested. "What if she's right where you left her? The witch and the old woman have kept you apart for so long. Don't help them. Don't hold yourself back because you're afraid."

CHAPTER 9

"YOU CAN COME out," Douglas said. "It's over."

Randy cautiously crawled from beneath the table after his dad signaled everything had gone back to normal in the library and they were out of danger.

"Good," Randy said. "Let's get the heck out of here. I'm starting to think the stories about this place are *true*."

The floor wasn't moving, not anymore, but the library looked like Dorothy's famous tornado had taken a wrong turn and torn through Astoria instead of the Kansas plains.

"It was an earthquake, son. That's all."

"Really?" Randy scanned the room and saw his book was buried beneath some rubble on the floor. He dug it out then shoved it into his father's hand.

"Look at this book!" Douglas gave his son a quizzical look before taking the leather-bound volume. "I'm telling you, Dad. This place isn't right!"

Douglas opened the book and began to flip nonchalantly through its pages. He didn't expect to find much, but his eyes registered surprise when he came to one of the book's early pages. "Well... I think I found your friends."

Randy wasn't sure what his father meant until he had the book back in his hands. He couldn't believe it. Douglas had stopped at one of the book's illustrations: a black-and-white sketch of Wesley and Taylor working to free the Tin Man! Somehow the kids from his class had become part of the book!

"Tell me, son. You want to see something cool?"

❖ ❖ ❖

The Munchkin maiden dragged a heavy log through the mud before struggling to place it on the chopping block. Once there, she gripped her axe, lifted it into the air, and brought it down on the log. She closed her eyes just as the blade struck only to open them a few seconds later and realize she'd barely made a dent.

"Ma'am?"

Startled, the maiden swung around to find three children standing near the old woman's well. There was a monster with them, a terrifying man made of metal who was holding an axe and had his eyes locked on the maiden.

"Oh, no! Get away! Please!" She stumbled over her feet. "Help! Someone! Please!" The maiden turned, running for the house, desperately hoping the old woman would allow her inside.

"Please!" The Tinman said. "Don't go!"

The sound of his voice was all the maiden needed. Her screams came to a halt, and she slowed to a stop, turning to study the four strangers once more.

"Nick? Is that... is it really..." She couldn't bring herself to finish but was already stepping toward them, her eyes fixed on the Tin Man's metal face. She was captivated by the man she'd feared just moments before. She put a hand to his cheek, but the Tin Man pulled away.

"Is it you?" she asked. "Is it really you?"

While reluctant, it was clear the Tin Man wouldn't escape without giving her the validation she needed. He turned to face her, finally giving in.

And when their eyes met—

"Oh my!" She wrapped her arms around the Tin Man and kissed his metal lips then moved her mouth from one side of his face to the other, peppering him with tiny, baby kisses. "Oh, My Love! My Love! I knew you'd come! I knew it!"

Wesley looked over at Taylor then let his gaze drop to her hand.

The maiden squealed with excitement, but the Tin Man pulled away. Tears were streaming down his face. He tried to wipe them away but panicked when he couldn't clear them with his metal hands.

"What's wrong?" the maiden asked.

"He's crying," Taylor explained.

"But they're tears of joy. I don't know if I'll ever stop crying them."

"He'll rust."

The Tin Man tried to respond but his jaw wouldn't move. Nothing came out but a hollow, *"Hmph!"* Just that quickly, his jaw had rusted shut again.

Wesley took the oil can from Locke. The Tin Man fell to one knee, allowing Wesley to grease the hinge in his jaw. He opened his mouth, testing it. Open. Closed. Open again. It creaked with each movement until the oil worked its way into the necessary joints.

When he was finished, the Tin Man turned away in an effort to hide his face. "I shouldn't have come. This was a mistake."

"Nonsense," the maiden said. She dropped to both knees beside him. "You promised to return no matter what, and you did. What else matters?"

"But the old woman—"

"We'll go far away. We'll never come back."

The hope in her voice touched Wesley on a level he didn't fully understand. Everything had gone wrong in her life. Someone had – quite literally – penned an unhappy ending for the maiden, and yet here she was, convinced she could make it better, convinced no one had more control over her life than she did.

The Tin Man's joints whined as he let his head hang. "People will talk," he said painfully. "What will you say when they laugh at you because you're married to a man without a heart?"

She came to her feet, looking down on her lover with pride. "I'll tell them they're wrong." She put a balled fist to her chest. "I'll tell them you have mine."

❖ ❖ ❖

Taylor and Locke sprinted through the meadow for the Tin Man's cabin in the distance. Wesley was struggling to keep up, the long grass and flowers clipping his ankles as he ran.

"You guys were right. Seeing them together like that..." Wesley's labored breaths wouldn't let him finish. He was wearing down, but he kept going. He could feel the sun's heat on his back. The yellow brick road whipped through the edge of his vision as he ran. He could hear the musical roar of the enormous waterfall in the distance. For the first time since his move to Astoria, Wesley Bates didn't feel the weight of a heavy heart in his chest. He wasn't worried about a thing. Not the bus ride to school or the locker room after gym, not the embarrassment of finding a seat in the cafeteria, not even Randy Stanford. He knew his life was still waiting on the other side of the portal, but all that mattered now were the hopeful thoughts of adventure bouncing around in his head.

The three friends continued through the meadow until Locke came to an abrupt halt and put an arm out to stop each of his friends. Wesley and Taylor were happy for the break. Both were sweating profusely and short on breath.

Locke pulled his dagger. "Pirates," he said. "Get ready."

Taylor grinned. "Locke, this isn't Neverland. I've read every *Oz* book in the series. There aren't any—"

A voice called out from the cabin, cutting Taylor off. "There you are! We were starting to worry."

Douglas Stanford stepped from inside the rickety building with his son. Just seeing the bully was enough to put that heavy weight in Wesley's chest again.

"I guess I've got good news and bad news," Douglas explained. "Which do you want first?" The kids didn't respond. "The good news is that two of you get to stay behind with your Uncle Douglas. The bad? Well, one of you has to go back through and tell that boring old fossil we have your friends." Douglas held out his arms as if offering nothing more than a welcome hug. "Who's staying?"

Taylor jabbed an angry finger at the man blocking their path. "There's three of us, and Locke's got a knife. We're all going home!"

Randy flinched, looking up at his dad with worry. Douglas only shrugged.

"He was hoping you'd say that. They're all yours, friend."

Wesley turned just as the shadowy figure appeared from the brush and descended upon them. The hooded man was impossibly quick, his gloved hands a blur as they grabbed Wesley and Taylor, tucking each of them under one of his lanky arms.

He grabbed at Locke next but got nothing but air when the Lost Boy evaded his grasp with a forward flip. Locke somersaulted through the air and landed in a crouched position just ahead of their attacker. From there he leapt, plunging his dagger into the hooded man's arm. The dark figure dropped both children, gripping his arm in pain and letting out a bone-chilling cry that seemed anything but human.

Locke took Taylor by the arm as Wesley rolled onto his side.

"Get her out of here!"

Wesley scrambled to his feet, but the cloaked man recovered in a flash. He snatched Wesley before he could escape, yanking him off his feet and pulling him into the air. Just like that, Wesley was face-to-face with the dark figure. Even this close, he couldn't quite make out the features beneath the hood. Instead, his gaze was locked on the hooded man's fiery eyes. Just inches away, he could hear the crackle of the flame; he could feel its heat. He kicked and swung – anything that might break the hooded man's iron grip. He closed his eyes, pushed back the man's hood, and began clawing at the dark figure's face. That was all it took. The cloaked man moved to protect himself, releasing Wesley and allowing him to fall to the ground.

Eyes open, Wesley was ready to take off again. He glanced back, only wanting to size-up his attacker once more before running to join his friends.

But what he saw left him frozen.

It left them *all* frozen.

There was a flaming Jack-O-Lantern on the hooded man's shoulders in place of a human head. The grotesque pumpkin was misshapen and appeared to be rotting despite the grim face cut into its flesh.

And that face.

If it had been carved into any other pumpkin – a pumpkin on someone's doorstep, perhaps – there would have been nothing particularly disturbing about it. It had a broad mouth with jagged teeth, oval eyes, and a nasal cavity that looked like the missing nose on the skeleton in Mr. Meadow's science class.

But it was the way the face *lived* that left Wes so unsettled. How that carved nose breathed air in-and-out. How the pumpkin's orange skin stretched and wrinkled with each movement. How those flaming eyes seemed to always be on you.

Taylor and Locke stared in disbelief. Even Randy was gaping, horrified by the monster that had finally been revealed.

Douglas laughed. "I'll assume you don't need me to introduce my friend."

Wesley crawled through the grass like a retreating crab as the Headless Horseman moved toward him. The Horseman extended a hand and his sword materialized in a flash of grey smoke.

All at once, the Tin Man's cabin filled with light.

Douglas wheeled around, his eyes filled with rage. "Don't even!"

Long pillars of light spilled through the cabin's windows. A blast of white shimmered through its open door. There was something moving around in the cabin too – a rail-thin shadow come to life.

The Librarian stepped through the door and into the meadow. He'd traded his bone-colored cane for a chiseled staff with a canary-colored stone at its tip. When they'd met him, The Librarian had leaned heavily on his cane. Now he was standing tall. Shoulders back. Chin up. He was a formidable opponent. If the old man's posture didn't give it away, the worry on Douglas's face certainly did.

"Wes!" Taylor yelled.

Wesley stumbled to his feet. The Horseman saw he was on the move and brought his sword down hard. Wesley didn't feel a thing when the blade sliced a shoelace that had come loose and was dragging behind him.

The Librarian waved the kids over. "Hurry, children! Hurry!"

Taylor and Locke went running for the cabin.

"Stop them!" Douglas barked. "Randy! Now!"

Randy snapped from his trance just as Wesley passed within reach. He grabbed him by the back of his shirt and yanked with such force the collar ripped and his knees buckled, sending Wesley to the ground once more.

Taylor and Locke reached the cabin's doorway and turned to see Wesley was caught. Locke moved to help, but The Librarian lowered his staff to stop him.

"What are you doing?" Taylor screamed. "He needs us!"

Behind them the light was already beginning to dissipate. "The portal's closing," the old man explained. "Your friend is on his own."

Randy pinned Wesley, rolled him over, then slung his body into the air, making sure the skinny kid would land on his back in the dirt. Wesley landed hard too, his face twisting with pain as the air went rushing out of his lungs.

Wesley turned over onto his stomach. Desperate, he tried to crawl away as quickly as he could.

Randy looked down on him with a smirk. "Like you could ever get away from me!" He grabbed Wesley at the ankles, ready to reel him in. Wesley clawed at the grass, his nails digging into the dirt, anything to delay the inevitable.

Randy leaned forward. He grabbed Wesley's shoulders and put his full weight behind both hands. On top of him now, Randy put a hand on the back of Wesley's head and smashed his face into the earth.

Taylor darted into the meadow. The Librarian grabbed her, struggling to hold Tay back as she swung her arms wildly at the air.

"Get your hands off him!" she screamed.

Locke watched in silence as Wesley twisted his neck so his face was no longer buried in the dirt. His glasses were crooked on his face, a twisted, mangled mess. Tears were welling up in his eyes. Blood was trickling from his nose.

"Good!" Douglas shouted. "Hold him still!"

"C'mon," Locke said quietly to himself. "You can take him, Wes."

Wesley spotted Locke, and the Lost Boy pumped his fist in the air.

"C'mon!" he cried. "You can take him!"

The defeat disappeared from Wesley's eyes. He braced his hand against the ground and pushed against the earth with every ounce of his strength. Randy stumbled back – no more than an inch, really – but enough to give Wesley the breathing room he needed. Wesley wiggled free and hurried to his feet. He turned to face Randy, a darkness in his eyes like angry thunderheads moving in from the horizon. But it was more than that. There was thunder and lightning, howling winds and pounding rain. There'd been a storm building inside of him since his first run in with Randy Stanford. It had been there, building in strength beneath the surface, hiding until now.

Randy sneered. "Look who's finally decided to—"

Wesley didn't let him finish. He balled his fingers into a tight fist and with one violent swing, the storm clouds burst, unleashing their fury onto the world. The blow landed flush across Randy's jaw, and the bully crumpled to the ground.

Wes stood over Randy, looking down in shock at what he'd done. His fist was cocked, ready to go again, but he couldn't keep it still. His hands were trembling.

The Librarian looked into the cabin. The light was already beginning to wane. "Come on!"

Wesley darted for the cabin. The Librarian quickly ushered Taylor and Locke through the door and into the light.

"Stop him!" Douglas was yelling at his son, but Randy didn't move. Furious, Douglas turned to the Horseman beside him. "Why are you even here?!"

The Horseman charged toward them, his sword poised for a violent thrust.

The Librarian saw him coming. The old man widened his stance and gripped his staff with both hands. *"Fulgur!"*

A bolt of yellow lightning surged from the stone atop The Librarian's staff, engulfed the Horseman, and sent him tumbling back the way he'd come.

Undeterred, the Horseman quickly came to his feet and closed on them again. He removed the Jack-O-Lantern from his shoulders and launched it through the air, throwing it at The Librarian so that a stream of orange fire trailed through the air behind it.

Wesley ducked under The Librarian's arm and into the cabin as the pumpkin drew near. The Jack-O-Lantern hit the door just as The Librarian pulled it shut. It tore the wooden door from its hinges, but the portal had closed.

The Librarian and the kids were gone.

CHAPTER 10

THE KIDS STOOD together, all three happy to see they were back in the library.

Taylor shot a look over her shoulder at the Oz carving then turned to face Wesley. "Oh my god! I can't believe you did that! Did you see the look on Randy's face? I told you he was all talk!"

Wesley forced a smile, but it disappeared in the tremble of his lips. A moment later, he burst into tears. All the emotions he'd bottled up since his move to Astoria – the sorrow, the anger, the loneliness and despair – they were all on display. He couldn't hold them back any longer. After all, once a rain cloud opens up like that, there's just no stopping it, no stopping it until all of the rain is gone.

❖ ❖ ❖

Still shaken, Randy watched as the Horseman came out of the cabin and re-attached his Jack-O-Lantern head.

Douglas snatched Randy by the arm and yanked him to his feet. "What were you thinking? How'd you let a scrawny little kid like that get the best of you?!"

"I... I..."

"Answer me!"

"Dad, I don't know. I'm sorry!"

Douglas studied his son through calmer eyes. "It's fine," he said. "I'm sorry, too. I shouldn't have yelled at you like that." He let go of Randy's arm. "I'm sure you'll get another shot at him."

He dusted off his son as the Horseman joined them. Randy was relieved to see he had pulled the hood back over his head.

"Right now we've got to move," Douglas explained. "We've got work to do, but we don't want to be out in the open like this when everything shifts."

Randy wiped his eyes. "What do you mean?"

"You'll see."

Randy watched Douglas take off his coat as he and the Horseman came together and started toward the tree line. Randy turned his attention on the empty cabin nearby. He could almost feel the tiny shack's pull on him, a quiet whisper calling out.

It's not safe with your dad. Not anymore.

Randy pushed the thought from his mind. The portal was closed. He couldn't go back even if he wanted to. And he didn't want to. He'd never join Wesley and Tay. They hated him. They wouldn't take him into their pathetic little group anyway.

You know that isn't true.

Randy hurried after Douglas and the Horseman. Things had gotten really weird, but he knew his dad would take care of him.

Will he?

"Shut up," Randy said. Douglas and the Horseman passed into the forest. Randy quickened his pace, following his dad deeper into Oz.

He had nowhere else to go.

❖ ❖ ❖

Wesley bent his glasses back into shape as he and the others followed The Librarian down one of the library's long aisles.

The old man was holding the dagger from the *Peter Pan* literature display loosely in his left hand. He hadn't said much since Locke explained what he'd seen and heard in Neverland. He was walking with a hunch, and Wesley noticed he occasionally had to use the bookcases for support as they moved through the stacks.

The Neverland carving was hanging at the end of the aisle, waiting.

"Here we are," The Librarian said.

He stepped back so Locke could say his goodbyes before heading home.

"You aren't coming with me?" Locke asked.

"Not yet," The Librarian explained.

"But what about Neverland? Hook says he's gotten help from someone in the real world to help him win the war. What's going to happen?"

"It's impossible to know just yet. I think it's pretty clear Douglas has traveled into a number of the storybook lands, but I can't do much for Neverland until I know exactly what he's done and, more importantly, what he has planned."

Taylor's eyes were already welling with tears when she turned to face Locke. "You could stay," she said desperately. "It's not as bad as it sounds. I promise. It would be something new everyday. And you could hang out with us on weekends. And we'd have classes together... and..."

"Take care of our guy," Locke said coolly. "Okay?"

She lunged forward and wrapped both arms around him. The move caught him off-guard, but he eventually allowed himself to sink into the warmth of her embrace.

Taylor let him go, wiping tears and missing the blush of embarrassment that tinged Locke's cheeks. She took a spot beside The Librarian, and he patted her on the back as Wesley moved toward their departing friend.

"Hey," Wesley began.

"Hey," Locke echoed.

"We're okay, right? I mean, we'll probably never see each other again, but... I need to know we're okay." Wesley lowered his gaze.

"It was an adventure, right?"

Wesley looked up. "Heck yeah!"

Locke offered his hand, and Wesley took it. The Lost Boy pulled him in for the kind of hug usually reserve for best friends.

"Good," Locke whispered into Wesley's ear. "Now go write another one."

They pulled apart. Wesley nodded.

Stand up for yourself, Wes.

Life's what you make it.

Believe in yourself.

Stop hiding who you really are.

Everyone in Wesley's life had been singing from the same hymn book for a long time now, but Locke had found a way to make the song his own.

Write your own story.

Wes finally understood.

Locke turned to The Librarian. Without a word, the old man approached the Neverland carving. He found the dagger-shaped tree hidden within the carving's forest and pushed the dagger into place. He stepped back, guiding Wesley and Taylor with him to make sure both were watching from a safe distance.

The carving began to shimmer. Then the tentacles appeared, reaching into the library and slowly wrapping themselves around Locke's tiny body.

The Lost Boy turned to face his friends.

The portal's light pulsed, growing so bright Taylor had to shield her eyes. So did the old man. But Wesley kept watching, just as reluctant to let go as Locke.

The fingers of light circled Locke, coiling around his legs, his torso, and his arms, until eventually his entire body was aglow.

Behind him, the carving was gone, nothing but white light where the chiseled landscape had been. As expected, the pool of light on the wall began to ripple and allowed them a quick glimpse into Neverland. There was a rocky cliff on the other side that overlooked a great lagoon. In the distance, two wooden ships were locked in an epic battle, their canons booming, their sails flapping in the wind. But Wesley didn't look. Even with the smell of gunpowder hanging in the air, even with the cool sea air stinging his face – Wesley kept his gaze fixed firmly on his friend.

Wesley raised his hand into the air, a motionless wave. Locke did the same.

"Goodbye," Locke whispered.

The light grew so intense Wesley saw little more than the dark silhouette of Locke's body. Then he couldn't see him at all. He couldn't see anything. Nothing but white.

"Goodbye... Locke Underfoot."

Moments later, the light dimmed and soon the world began to take shape around Wesley once more. The bookcases were first to appear – then a desk nearby. Taylor and The Librarian came into view just after that, and eventually the light waned enough that Wesley could see the pool of light hanging on the stone wall ahead of him. But there was nothing standing between him and the carving as the tentacles began to recede into the wood-work.

Wesley's new friend was gone.

CHAPTER 11

"YOU OKAY?" TAYLOR asked.

Wesley was biting at his lip. "Yeah, I think so."

The Librarian walked with them into the main hall and toward the library's lobby. "Can I assume you children know not to talk about what you've seen here today?"

"Of course," Wesley said. "But... what *did* we see? I mean... what the heck is going on around here?"

Taylor winced at his tone and tried to let Wesley know he'd crossed a line. "Wesley?"

"I'm sorry, it's just—"

"It's a great deal to take in," the old man agreed.

Wesley looked down at The Librarian's burned arm. "Why were they doing that to you?"

"And how does Randy's dad know about Oz?" Taylor added.

"Who was that with him? Was that the Headless Horseman? I mean... for real?"

"It's nothing you need to concern yourselves with."

"But maybe we can help," Wesley said.

The Librarian looked down his long nose at the boy. "Did you children meet anyone while in Oz? Did you talk with any of the people there?"

Wesley gave Taylor a chance to speak up before answering himself. "Locke told us we weren't allowed."

The old man looked about at the wreck his library had become. He walked over to a desk where he righted a chair that had fallen in the quake then replaced a lamp that had fallen to the floor. "Tell me why you want to help."

Wesley let his eyes fall to the floor. "I can't explain it, but I knew the minute I stepped off the bus. It's like I moved to Astoria just so I could find this place. I write stories about places like this."

"You're a writer?"

Taylor answered for him. "That's like calling a river wet. It's all he does. He's always scribbling in his notebook and reading books most kids our age have never even heard of. He was excited about this trip all week, and that was before he found out about all this."

The old man stroked the length of his beard. "I see," he said. "Wait here."

The Librarian disappeared for a moment. When he returned, he was carrying a large leather-bound book with a thick red ribbon hanging from its gilt pages.

"Take this," The Librarian explained.

Wesley tried to wave the gift off. "Oh no! I couldn't!"

"Of course you can! Besides, I think you might find something of interest hidden within its pages."

Wesley took the book. "Like what?" he asked.

"We'll leave that for another day."

Curious, Wesley watched The Librarian tell Taylor goodbye. Was there something waiting for him in the book? Something he was supposed to find? He didn't want to start flipping through the book's pages just yet, but something told him he had another mystery to add to his list.

The kids started for the exit. "Be safe out there," The Librarian said, waiting for them to disappear into the lobby. "Come back. But please... be safe."

❖ ❖ ❖

Wesley and Taylor walked through the lobby, both a little hesitant to go outside; they understood they'd be in a lot of trouble for disappearing on Ms. Easton like they had. And that was hours ago. Neither had a clue what was waiting for them outside the library doors.

"You sure you're okay?" Taylor asked.

"I'm fine. Why do you keep asking that?"

"I don't know. I just... why were you crying? Randy's been bullying you since your first day. I don't get it. I thought you'd do a little dance after punching his lights out like that."

He shook his head. "I didn't punch his lights out, Tay. It wasn't like I imagined, either. Besides, you didn't give *Locke* a hard time when *he* was crying."

Taylor let her expression soften. "You mean when you jumped in front of his knife to save me?"

Wesley pushed the library's heavy door open. Early evening light poured into the building. "How many times have you jumped in to save me, Taylor?"

She studied her friend. There was a confidence in his eyes that she'd never seen before. He seemed so adult. A chill ran the length of Taylor's spine. Her skin felt funny, too. Hot and tingly. It was like something they said had charged the air around them with electricity.

Maybe it was the way he had called her Taylor.

"Where have you two been?"

Both children looked up with a start. Two police cars were idling near the school bus, their red and blue lights flashing. Ms. Easton marched up the walk toward them, an adult couple on her left and a graying man in oil-stained overalls on her right.

"Is that—"

"Our parents!" Wesley couldn't believe it. "We're in some serious—"

Wesley's mother grabbed him before he could finish. Taylor's father had her by the arm, too. Just like that, their parents were pulling them apart.

Neither one had a chance to say goodbye.

The electricity between them was gone.

CHAPTER 12

WESLEY SAT ON the edge of his bed and thumbed through a new comic he'd bought on Wednesday. It was late. There was an untouched plate of food on his desk: potatoes and pot roast. His father had sent him to his room for the evening. It wasn't much of a punishment, but no one in the house could remember the last time Wesley was grounded which left them with little experience to draw on.

"...and I don't want you hanging out with that Taylor Morales," Wesley's mom had told him. "She's a bad influence. I've been saying that all along."

That was his real punishment. And truthfully, it didn't make any sense. His mom loved Tay, always had. Wesley couldn't understand why she was pinning everything that happened on her.

Nervous energy sent Wes bouncing around his room like a ping pong ball. He traded the comic for his video game before tossing that aside a few minutes later in favor of the action figures kept in a box under his bed. But even they couldn't hold his attention long. They just weren't enough. His toys, his games, his whole world – everything seemed so ordinary.

Wesley slapped at a basketball on the floor beside him. It came to life with a hop, and he smacked it again. This time it bounced just out reach and rolled across the room before coming to rest near the *Oz* book The Librarian had given him. He crawled across the room and picked the book up. He'd forgotten The Librarian's words...

Did you find anything hidden within its pages?

He flipped through the book and found a long metal bookmark lying between its parchment pages. A red ribbon was looped through a hole punched into the bookmark's tip. There were a number of strange markings etched into the metal like hieroglyphics. He recognized one of the symbols immediately: an open book with lines radiating from its pages. The same symbol from the carvings in the library.

That's it? Wesley thought. *A freakin' bookmark?*

He hung the bookmark around his neck like a medallion then began digging deeper into the book. A smile appeared as he carefully began to turn the book's aged pages, but the broad grin quickly vanished when he found what was waiting within. Each page brought an expression to his face that was more troubled than the last until eventually he was frantically flipping to the back of the book.

Wesley jumped to his feet, set the book down, and pulled a walkie-talkie from his backpack. He hurried across the room, opened his window, then extended the antenna on his walkie and turned it on. "Tay? Tay, you there?"

A window shade popped open in the house directly behind the Bates' home. Taylor appeared behind the glass, a walkie-talkie of her own in hand.

"So what happened? They gonna ship you off to military school?"

"What? No! My dad sent me to my room for the night. What about you?"

Taylor didn't answer right away. "I don't know. It was weird. My dad didn't say a word the whole way home. Not a thing. He didn't even ground me."

"I wonder…"

"What?"

"Never mind," he said. "You have to see this."

Wesley grabbed the book and placed it in a small Easter basket made of wire mesh. Shortly after they met, Wesley and Taylor had spent a long weekend building an elaborate contraption that allowed them to pass items back-and-forth from his window to hers. It wasn't pretty. Actually, made from jump ropes, holey bed sheets, and a coil of rubber tubing they'd found at an abandoned construction site, it was something of an eyesore. Their parents were constantly threatening to take it down, but never did, which was good, because tonight Wesley needed the ugly rig more than ever.

He hooked the basket to the pulley system and began pulling on a rope that took the basket through the air. He held his breath as the *Oz* book dangled precariously over the above-ground pool in the Bates' backyard as he sent it to Taylor.

❖ ❖ ❖

Across town, The Librarian gently rubbed salve on his arm then wrapped it tightly in thin, white gauze. He already knew the burn the Horseman left would leave a sizeable scar. Parallel stripes where his bony fingers had gripped The Librarian's arm would serve as a constant reminder of his run-in with the ghastly apparition. The Horseman, infamous for tormenting the people of Sleepy Hollow, had another black deed on his record now. And likely more to come.

It's appropriate, The Librarian told himself. *Perhaps I need something to help me remember what can happen when one of my students is led astray.*

He stood from his chair, joints cracking as his weary bones moaned in protest. His body needed rest, but he had more pressing concerns. The way the library shook earlier – he knew better than to call it an earthquake – meant he had a long and treacherous journey ahead of him.

The Librarian eased toward his desk, moving around the downed bookcase and the battered portrait of Mark Twain on the floor. He struggled to push his large, wooden desk across the room. There was a loose tile in the floor beneath it. The old man pried it up and revealed a small nook filled with strange crystals, bottled powders, and potions.

❖ ❖ ❖

Taylor anxiously pulled the *Oz* book from the basket then sat down beneath her window and began to flip through its pages. "Oh my god, Wes!"

"Are you looking?" Wesley's voice crackled from the walkie-talkie resting on Taylor's window-sill. She'd found the illustration Randy spotted earlier and was amazed to see that she and her friends had become part of the story. Her heart was racing. There was something about it that excited her, knowing they'd taken some of the library's magic home with them. But digging deeper revealed a second illustration, one that showed Dorothy traveling down the yellow brick road with two companions. The Cowardly Lion was there. So was the Scarecrow. The Tinman, however, was missing. She flipped further into the book and found Dorothy and her friends being chased by an immense swarm of giant bees.

"Tay? You there?"

She ignored him, a flicker of realization in her eyes. She knew the *Oz* mythos well. In the book, she knew it was the Tin Man who saved Dorothy and her friends from the bee attack. But the metal man they'd met didn't seem to be part of this strange new version of the classic tale. Not at all.

Taylor reluctantly let herself turn to the back of the book. The book's final illustration showed the Wicked Witch standing over Dorothy Gale's dead body. Taylor's eyes fixed on the rotten teeth in the witch's smile. Suddenly shaken, she tossed the book across the room and grabbed her walkie-talkie.

"Wes! You don't think—"

"That we changed the story? What else could it be? Look through your other stuff. Your *Oz* stuff. Maybe it's just The Librarian's book."

Taylor sprang to her feet, angry she hadn't thought of that first. She tore across her room and found the beloved book her mother had spent so many nights reading to her. She sped through the worn pages. Everything had changed, just like The Librarian's copy. Even the cover featured the Wicked Witch, as if the ugly woman were the story's heroine instead of Dorothy in her blue and white dress.

The book fell from Taylor's trembling hand. Her throat tightened.

Wesley's voice sounded through the hiss of static. "Well?"

Taylor stumbled back to the window and grabbed her walkie. She was scared. Seeing Wesley across the way helped curb her fears but not nearly enough. She wanted to be over there with him. "My mom's book changed, too."

"Jeez!"

"What does that mean?"

"It means we have to go back, Tay." He wanted to elaborate but couldn't find the words, all he could do was repeat himself. "We have to go back."

❖ ❖ ❖

The Librarian came down the stairs and saw that night shadows had overtaken every inch of his library. He walked over to the *Oz* display and took the wand from its pedestal before starting down the aisle and towards the mystical piece of art that would allow him to return to the fairy tale land. When he arrived, the old man placed the wand into the carving just as Locke had before. He allowed it to click into place then stepped back and let out a quiet sigh as light from the carving began to envelop his frail body.

Moments later, The Librarian was back in the Tin Man's cabin. The shack's door was lying on the floor after being ripped from its hinges. From where he stood the open door already allowed a glimpse into Oz; it was enough to confirm his worst fears were true.

The old man cautiously stepped into the meadow. Gloom washed over him when he saw what had become of the storybook land. The sky was dark with an army of winged monkeys flying overhead. Trees were dying, their dry branches skeletal and barren. He heard frightened screams calling from deep within the forest. The yellow brick road lay in ruins, snaking its way through the scorched earth that was once the lush meadow where so much of the children's adventure had taken place. In the distance, the old man could see the remains of Emerald City crumbling to the ground. He'd arrived just in time to witness the last of the reset – the last of the shift.

The Librarian took a deep breath as he began his journey into Oz. He understood the long odds he faced in the battle to come. He knew exactly what had happened...

Evil had taken over.

AKNOWLEDGEMENTS

I'll be the first to admit there are better writers in the world, but no one has a support system like mine...

To my mother: thank you for taking the time to convince me I had a novel in me. I often try to emulate other authors in my work, but your voice has had more influence on my prose than anyone else's. Working on this one together is something I'll cherish for a long time to come.

To my father: you'll never understand how influential you've been in all my endeavors. You've always supported my decision to walk a different path than the one you envisioned, and the example you set in your life has always been the guiding light when I was tempted by distractions or shortcuts that promised an easier way. I doubt I'll ever work as hard as you did, but I'll give it a shot.

To my children: you've never been embarrassed to let me play with you like I was just another kid in the neighborhood. You'll always be the audience I'm most desperate to impress. You're the light of my life, and it's already tough to envision a time when you're both out in the world chasing dreams of your own. I'll miss you more than you'll ever know so don't be sad when you feel my hands on your back as I push you out of the house. You have to chase your dreams when you're young and fearless. It's time to chase yours now.

And finally, to my wife: you believed in me long before you should have, convinced I would eventually write something people wanted to read. Ironically, that never would have happened without you. Your undying belief in me has always made me feel like I was strong enough to take on the world. I can't tell you how happy I am we get to take it on together.

ALSO BY ERIC HOBBS

<u>The Librarian</u>
Little Boy Lost
Unhappily Ever After

<u>Nightcrawler Tales</u>
The Bandage Man
Open House
88 Keys

<u>Comics & Graphic Novels</u>
The Broadcast
Once Upon a Time Machine
Batman: Intervention

ABOUT THE AUTHOR

Since his debut, Eric Hobbs has seen his work published by DC Comics, Dark Horse, and NBM. His debut graphic novel, *The Broadcast*, was nominated for the ALA's annual "Great Graphic Novels for Teens" list before being named "Graphic Novel of the Year" by influential website Ain't It Cool News. *The Librarian* is his first novel.

erichobbsonline.com
facebook.com/erichobbs